WHAT AM I?

Using the Book

This book can be read like a normal book. However, to make it more interesting, we have included a flap at the end. Use this flap to make a game out of the book.

Each page has four chunks of information on one place. Use the flap to show just one info block at a time, and try to identify the object or instrument first and then who made it or invented it first. The fourth clue more or less tells you the name of the object or instrument. Below the info blocks, you can see a picture connected to the object or instrument and read some more about it.

Fold the sheet to show clues as shown in the figures.

Fold once to show the first clue. Able to guess the object and answer it correct? Are you related to Thomas Edison or what? Get 20 points.

Fold again to show the second clue. Correct answer? Get 15 points. Your brain deserves to be kept in a museum.

Fold to show the third clue. A correct answer at this stage gets you 10. You may not be Edison but you are a close cousin.

No answers as yet? Fold again to show the fourth clue. This one was plain unlucky for you. Take 5, if you answer it here.

No answers? Guess what? You are actually the luckiest! You don't get any point, but you get to see the picture of the object or instrument and read some interesting tidbits about it.

Talk to Us

We invite readers to compile pieces of information in the style followed in this book. Try to keep some information that is interesting and seldom heard of apart from the usual necessary information. Do not forget to include your source for the information. Send this to us with your name and address, and we will include it in an upcoming edition of the book, with your name as a contributor.
So what are you waiting for? Get up and get cracking.

WHAT AM I?

100 Historic Inventions and Discoveries of the World

Nellie Dhillon
Don Bosco School, New Delhi

wisdom tree

This book is a compilation of facts and information from various sources. However, the figures and numbers given in this work are subject to change according to time. Care has been taken to verify the contents very thoroughly up to the time of publication. In case anyone has any query, clarification, complaint, or suggestion, please let us know, and we will immediately look into it. Also, in case anyone feels a credit is due, immediately write to us, and we will get back to you. Any infringement of copyright or trademark is not intended.

First published 2004
Reprinted 2005, 2006, 2008, 2009, 2011, 2013

ISBN: 978-81-86685-82-2

Published by
Wisdom Tree,
4779/23, Ansari Road,
Darya Ganj, New Delhi-110002
Ph.: 23247966/67/68
wisdomtreebooks@gmail.com

Printed in India

Introduction

Existence or survival depends on learning to live with Nature. The early man lived a life of a nomad, wandering from place to place in search of food and shelter. Somewhere down the line, man in his attempt to understand Nature, developed the desire to invent new things or objects that would make life a bit easier. Beginning with the discovery of fire and invention of the wheel, man advanced further and today, we are witness to Space Age and Information Technology revolution. Yet, many doubts linger — 'how', 'when', 'where', 'why' and 'what' are frequent queries that continue to haunt the scientifically inclined. And due to rejection of theories until scientifically and physically verified, the queries and their answers become a brilliant exercise in logic, observation and experimentation.

The famous Greek scientist, Archimedes, was asked to find out *what* was the weight of the king's crown that was made of pure gold. He wondered and pondered over the problem till one day, while lowering himself into the bathtub, he saw the water level rise. He leapt out and ran stark naked in the street, shouting, "*Eureka*!" ("I've found it"). He deduced the principle that a body in water displaced the same amount of water as its weight. Thus, it is the query '*what*' that has led to many a great discovery and invention. This book is meant to satisfy the curiosity of young minds on *what* are the many useful objects found in everyday life, *what* they are made of, *what* led to their discovery or invention. What is more, you will find answers to many other questions this 100-page book raises.

I have attempted to bring together different man-made objects based on such varied disciplines as physics, chemistry, medical science, biochemistry, etc. and used in equally varied fields like photography, arms manufacture, tailoring, preservation of food, nutrition and in other spheres of life. Hence, you will find information on thermometers, airconditioners, aspirin, writing objects, fibre optics, sewing machines, radio, contact lens, compass, gunpowder and a whole gamut of materials used in making our life so easy and convenient. Not only will this book serve as a small (small, because it is not possible to cover all the objects used in life in one such volume) treasure-house of information, it may even encourage some of the creative and scientifically inclined readers to find out *what* makes the world tick around us.

Nellie Dhillon

I am probably one of the most used and ignored inventions of all times. I was invented in 1930 by 3M engineer, Richard Drew, who had earlier invented the first masking tape. Drew joined 3M, the company making sandpaper. He noticed car painters having a hard time making clean dividing lines on two-colour paint jobs. He then invented the world's first masking type of me with adhesive on the edges.

I was originally intended for sealing bakery and grocery products. As demand went down during the depression in these industries, I was lapped up by regular American consumers, who discovered that they could use me to mend torn pages, broken toys, ripped window shades, and even dilapidated currency. I could also be used for sticking envelopes and putting up posters.

I am nearly invisible, waterproof, transparent and made from oils, resins and rubber. I have a coated cellophane backing. My brand name came about while Drew was testing his first masking tape to determine how much adhesive he needed to add. The body shop painter became frustrated with the sample masking tape and exclaimed, "Take this tape back to those Scotch bosses of yours and tell them to put more adhesive on it!"

My inventor, Drew, heard that an insulation firm needed help with a waterproof covering for **insulation batts** that it was designing. A colleague of his was thinking of packaging 3M masking tape rolls in cellophane, which was a new moisture-proof wrap created by DuPont. "Why not directly coat cellophane with adhesive?" Drew remarked. And I was born. I am the world's first waterproof, see-through, pressure-sensitive tape.

Cellophane Tape or Clear Adhesive Tape

This is the cellophane or the adhesive tape. John A. Borden, another 3M engineer, invented the first tape dispenser with a built-in cutter blade in 1932. Scotch™ Magic™ Transparent Tape was invented in 1961. This was an almost invisible tape that never discoloured and could be written on.

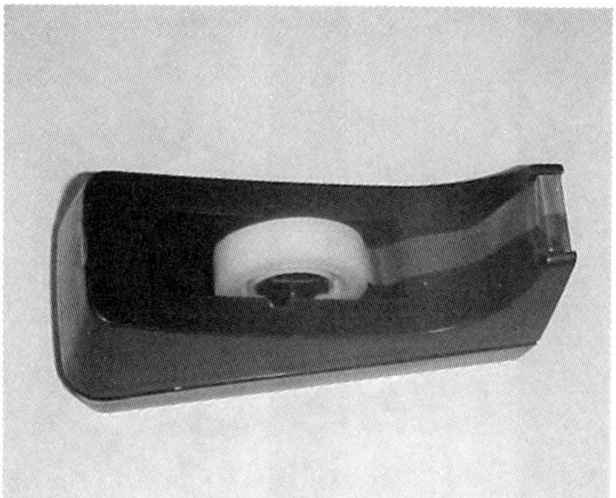

I am not a very new invention as far as the idea goes. I am not the work of one, but of many scientists. However, the man who turned scientific thought so as to bring me about can be said to be an Italian scientist, Santorio Santorio. Santorio Santorio was one of a group of learned men in Venice who connected the phenomenon of expansion of air to the increase in temperature. He also applied a scale to the whole system.

My first development phase can be credited to Galileo, who took a small rounded glass flask with a neck about 16 ins. long. He warmed the flask well in his hands, then turned its mouth upside down into a vessel placed underneath, in which there was a little water. When he removed his hands from the flask, the water at once began to rise in the neck. He then made use of this effect to build an instrument for checking whether something was hotter or colder than another.

The **thermoscope** invented by Galileo was given a numerical scale by Santorio Santorio. It thus became a full-fledged air temperature measuring device. The Grand Duke of Tuscany, Ferdinand II, filled my ancestor with alcohol. It thus became more respectable. However, this instrument made by him was not accurate.

Gabriel Fahrenheit was the one who brought me to my present form, as you know me today. He used a semi-solid inside me and I became most accurate in telling temperature differences and measuring temperatures. He also discovered and devised the first standard temperature scale for me. Fahrenheit divided the freezing and boiling points of water into 180 degrees.

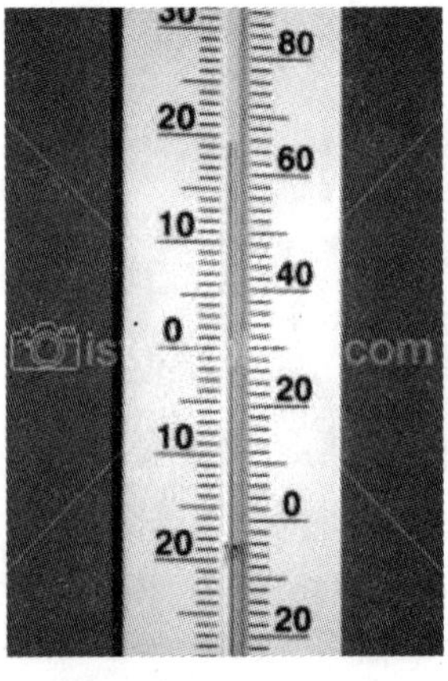

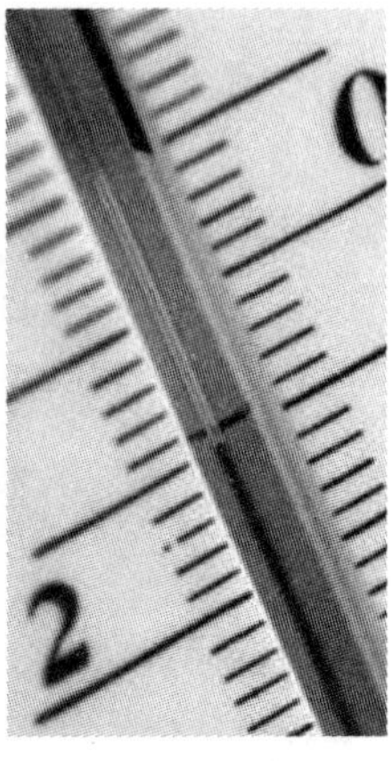

Mercury Thermometer

This is the mercury thermometer. Of the three universal temperature scales discovered, the Fahrenheit and Celsius systems are still in use and are considered the standard scientific temperature scales. The Celsius scale was developed by Anders Celsius.

I first started operating in 1902 in a Brooklyn printing plant. The printing-press owner was very concerned about the fluctuations in heat and humidity in his plant, which altered the dimensions of paper. However slight the change was, it was enough to cause misalignment of the coloured inks. My inventor had graduated just a year ago from Cornell University in engineering, and was employed at the Buffalo Forge Company on a starting salary of $10 per week.

I created a stable environment and the four-colour printing jobs taken up by the firm became aligned. Soon, industries manufacturing film, tobacco, processed meats, medical capsules, textiles, etc. took me up and saw significant improvements in quality. My inventor, Willis Haviland Carrier, and six other engineers formed a corporation in 1915 with a starting capital of $35,000. The company was dedicated to improving air-treatment technology.

According to Carrier, my idea came to him while waiting for a train. He immediately drew me on a napkin so that he would not forget how to make it. By the time the train arrived, he understood the relationship between temperature, humidity and dew point. Carrier spoke to the American Society of Mechanical Engineers about his basic rational **psychometric formula**, which is till today the basis of all fundamental calculations for the industry that makes me.

In 1921, Carrier improved on my design to include a **centrifugal refrigeration** system. I thus became the first practical method of cooling large spaces. Cooling for human comfort, rather than industrial need, began in 1924 by three Carrier centrifugal chillers installed in the J.L. Hudson Department Store in Detroit, USA. Shoppers flocked to the store. In 1928, Carrier gave me a form for private home use and called it the 'Weathermaker'.

Airconditioner

This is the 'airconditioner' which was introduced by textile engineer, Stuart H. Cramer, who used the phrase in a 1906 patent claim filed for a device that added water vapour to the air in textile plants. Carrier invented and patented 80 different airconditioners and is known as the 'father of the cool'. The company started by him, Carrier Engineering Corporation, is still the largest seller of airconditioners.

I am an instrument that measures altitude in comparison to a fixed reference level. Louis Paul Cailletet, a French physicist was the first to invent me. Usually, there are two types of me. One form deduces the altitude as well as the atmospheric pressure. My use is limited to measuring the altitude only above sea level and not above other natural land features such as mountains. In 1928, Paul Kollsman, a German inventor gave me my most accurate **barometric** form.

Since I measure atmospheric pressure, I am widely used in airplanes, hot air ballooning and mountain climbing. Popularly referred to as the 'Kollsman Window', I made a huge impact in the world of aviation. With my assistance the pilots are able to adjust the atmospheric pressure in flight. My advent helped in providing better aviation safety and in establishing routine flight schedules, all around the world. Kollsman was awarded the Guggenheim Medal for his very important contribution to aeronautics.

In 1924, Lloyd Espenschied invented my other form: my radar form. My first public demonstration was in New York, in 1938. I transmit radio signals that bounce off the ground, which are then picked up by a receiver in the aircraft. The total time taken by the radio signals after they have been transmitted and received is converted into absolute altitude. I am used in the automatic landing systems of aerospace vehicles.

I am of great use in military aircraft that have to fly in low altitudes at extremely high speeds. I can also measure altitudes from a remote spacecraft by bouncing beams of light from the earth surface back to the spacecraft. This information combined with the radial orbit knowledge helps to determine the **topography** of the earth's surface. I am used even while skydiving to enable the skydiver to quickly ascertain the changes in altitude so as to avoid the danger zones.

Altimeter

I am an altimeter. The bumps and dips on the earth's topography can be measured with the help of an altimeter fitted on to a remote satellite. A laser altimeter can measure height from a spacecraft above an ice sheet.

I am a service that is very essential for medical treatment or help. I was conceived in Europe by the Knights of St. John during the **Crusades** of the 11th century, who acted as the first emergency workers. They gave first-aid and medical treatment to soldiers of both sides and took the wounded to nearby tents for further treatment. At the same time, soldiers who carried the other wounded soldiers in for medical treatment were paid small amounts.

The first systematic development of me was by Surgeon-in-Chief of the French Grand Army, Baron Dominiquie Larrey, who created the first official army medical corp, in 1792. Trained medical personnel went into the battlefield to give first-aid to the wounded. Some were carried back to the medical tents by stretchers, hand-drawn carts and wagons to the field hospitals.

In 1870, 160 wounded soldiers were taken out of the fields by air balloons during Prussian **siege of Paris**, signifying my first use in air. In the 1950s, the United States used helicopters for my purpose during the Korean war. Initially only used during war, I began to be used for civilian purposes by mid 19th century in New York City. While palanquins or coolies were used in India, wicker cradles, called mule panniers and camel litters, were used in Egypt.

All my vehicles today are required to have certain basic equipment to give emergency medical treatment. In 1792, Dominique-Jean Larrey came up with the idea of light-weight, two-wheeled vehicles that allowed surgeons to work on the battlefield. The horse-drawn carriages had a moveable floor that could be drawn out for the patient. Beneath the driver's seat is a medical kit with brandy, **tourniquets**, bandages, sponges, blankets and persulphate of iron.

Ambulance Service

The world's oldest ambulance manufacturers are Hess and Eisenhardt in Cincinnati, Ohio, USA. The ambulances were built with medicine cabinets, roof lights and two-way radios. In 1937, they sold the first airconditioned ambulance built in America. The first British civilian air ambulance service started serving the Scottish Isles, in 1933, formally heralding the ambulance service.

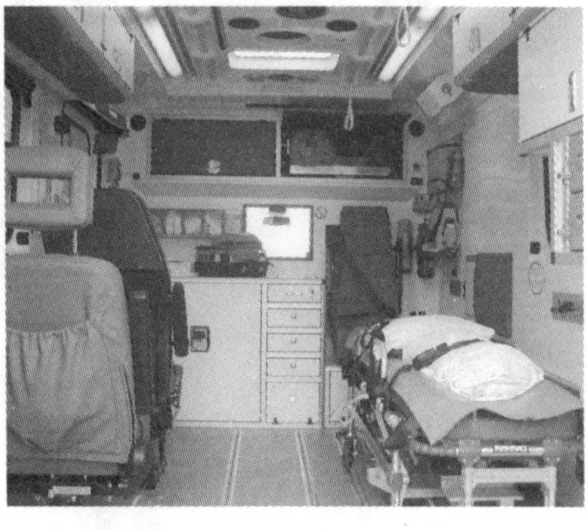

Inside of an ambulance.

I used to be called a dynamo. My work involves converting mechanical energy into electrical energy. Electricity is an important form of energy that is widely used. My work revolves around the phenomenon caused by the relation between magnetism and electricity. An electric conductor creates an electric current as it moves across a magnetic field. The electric utility power stations use either turbines or engines to get me working.

In the electric utility industries, I contain a magnet that is attached to the end of a rotating shaft. This magnet is then suspended inside a stationary conducting ring. A long wire is wrapped around this ring. As the magnet rotates, it creates an electric current in each section of the wire. Each section contains small electrical conductors. All the small currents are then added up to form one high-magnitude electric current.

In 1831-1832, Michael Faraday built my first electromagnetic form that consisted of a copper disc that would rotate between the poles of a horseshoe. In 1832, Hippolyte Pixii, a French instrument maker, built my first dynamo form. There was one major drawback in both these designs. They would produce sudden spikes of the current and sometimes none at all. Antonio Pacinotti, an Italian scientist, settled this problem. He replaced the spinning coil with a **toroidal** one.

Zenobe Gramme reinvented this design and named me Gramme dynamo. Though there have been many changes: the core idea of using a spinning loop of wire has remained in all the recent designs. I would create an electric current and not an electric charge. Before the electromagnetic phenomenon was discovered, a British inventor, James Wimhurst, built the Wimhurst machine based on **electrostatic principles**.

Electric Generator

This is the electric generator. Michael Faraday of England and Joseph Henry of USA separately built the first laboratory models of the electric generator in 1832. Hippolyte Pixii of France built a hand-driven model of an electric generator in 1833. Nikola Tesla of America built the first alternating-current generator in 1892.

I have been man's most significant invention since I eventually brought about the industrial revolution. The advent of any mechanised system without me or the design of a balanced component that moves in a circular motion on an axis would not have been possible. The tiny gears inside a watch as also the automobiles, jet engines and computer disk drives — all use the same principle.

Ancient clay tablets act as a proof to my earliest known use as a potter's wheel. My past was traced back to Ur in Mesopotamia, around 3500 BC. There is speculation on whether I was used for industrial and commercial purposes first and then on vehicles. I first had spokes and was used on Egyptian chariots around 2000 BC. I was then developed in Europe around 1400 BC. I have a very simple design and presumably every civilisation had developed me or used me in some way.

In highly developed civilisations like the great Inca, Aztec and Mayan civilisations, I was never used. There has been no evidence whatsoever of my use among the native inhabitants of the Western Hemisphere. This did happen but only after my widespread use in Europe, where very little development of my design and use occurred. Only around the beginning of the 19th century did I start evolving.

I was being used in a great many ways. I came equipped in thousands of different mechanisms. The industrial revolution reinforced my status as the most important component of technology. Through the many millennia of the Paleolithic period and the Neolithic period, no use of me was known to humans. My use was not known to native Americans until the Europeans introduced me.

Wheel

This is the wheel. In the Old World it came into use in the Bronze Age, when oxen and horses were first used as draft animals. It was later that the wheeled vehicles were devised.

I am the gear required for deep-sea diving. I consist of one or more gas tanks strapped to the diver's back, connected to an air hose and an invention called the demand regulator. The demand regulator controls the flow of air, so that the air pressure within the diver's lungs equals the pressure of the water. Emile Gagnan and Jacques Cousteau invented the demand regulator and the autonomous diving suit.

Divers probably began using **snorkels** made of hollow reeds around AD 100, as the first piece of equipment. By 1300, Persian divers were using underwater eye-goggles, made from polished shells or tortoises. In the 16th century, barrels were used as primitive diving bells, and for the first time divers could travel underwater with more than one breath of air, but not much more than one.

In 1771, British engineer, John Smeaton invented the air pump. A hose was connected between the air pump and the diving barrel, allowing air to be pumped to the diver. In 1772, a Frenchman, Sieur Freminet invented a 'rebreathing' device that recycled the exhaled air from inside the barrel. The invention was a poor one and the inventor died from lack of oxygen after being in his own device for 20 minutes.

In 1825, English inventor, William James designed another self-contained breather — a cylindrical iron 'belt' attached to a copper helmet. The belt held about 450 psi (pressure per square inch) of air, enough for a seven-minute dive. In 1876, an Englishman, Henry Fleuss invented a closed circuit, oxygen rebreather. Fleuss decided to use his invention for a 30-ft deep dive underwater. He died from inhaling the pure oxygen; oxygen is toxic to humans under pressure.

Scuba Diving Suit

This is the scuba diving suit. In 1873, Benoît Rouquayrol and Auguste Denayrouze built a new piece of equipment, with a perfected air supply, and a total weight of 85 kg. Famous magician, Harry Houdini, in 1921, invented a 'diver's suit' that allowed divers, in case of danger, to quickly divest themselves of the suit while submerged and to safely escape and reach the surface of water.

In ancient times, herbalists would prescribe my natural form that would be found in the bark of the willow tree or in the leaves of the wintergreen or meadowsweet plants. My active ingredient is acetyl salicylic acid that is a derivative of salicylic acid. For a long time I was a natural remedy for curing minor aches and pains. Hippocrates, the father of modern medicine, had studied and used my powder form to fix headaches, joint pains and fever.

My use had declined as the years went by. However, in 1838, Raffaela Piria, an Italian chemist started experiments on me. He was able to break the salicin compound found in willow plants into sugar and salicylaldehyde. Through the processes of **hydrolysis** and oxidation, he converted this into salicylic acid. One major drawback was that salicylic acid was tough on the stomach lining. In 1853, Carl Frederic Gerhardt, a French chemist, was able to synthesise acetyl salicylic acid artificially for the first time.

This discovery augmented my production and widespread use. In 1899, Felix Hoffman, a German chemist who worked at Friedrich Bayer & Co., was the one who rediscovered my formula and used me to help his father who was suffering from arthritis. Bayer then later patented me. I was initially sold in a powdered form. I curb the production of prostaglandins in the body. I do not fix the problem but instead work on lowering the pain signals.

As I go into the stomach and get digested, I enter the bloodstream and this way go through the entire body. I then work my magic wherever prostaglandins are produced. In some cases, prostaglandins form blood clots that can even cause heart attacks. I have shown promise in solving various problems such as cataracts, cancer, gum disease and the incidence of high blood pressure in pregnant women. I am one of the world's safest and least expensive pain-relievers with over 100 years of proven track record.

Aspirin

Aspirin was the original brand name given to acetyl salicylic acid by the Bayer Company in Germany. Its first use can be dated back to ancient Greece.

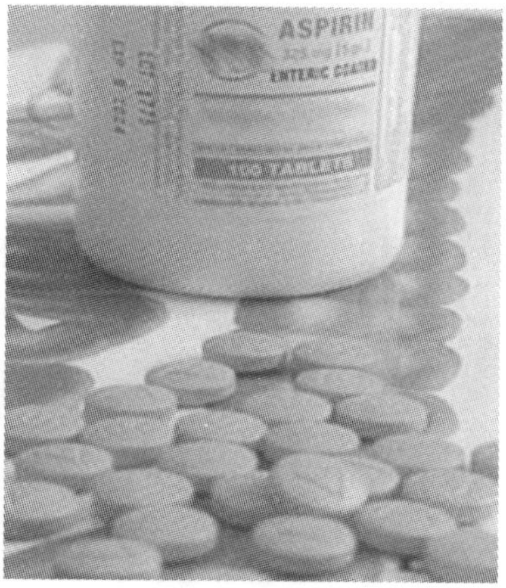

I replaced the quill. I was built in such a way that I would carry my own supply of ink. With my advent there was no problem about constantly dipping the quill into the inkwell, splattering or smearing ink. I consist of a nib. The feed or the black part built under the nib keeps a control over the ink flow. This nib, when it comes in contact with the paper, writes on it. In my earlier designs, I could be refilled by using an eyedropper.

Later I was designed to have a self-filling flexible rubber sac that would work like a pump and suck in the ink on being dipped into an inkwell. I have nine different nib sizes along with three different tip cuts. Lewis Waterman, an insurance salesman, patented my first practical form. He got inspired to make an improvement of my existing form after he destroyed an important insurance document with a leaky pen. He added a hole in the nib and three grooves inside the feed.

Laszlo Biro, a Hungarian journalist, along with his brother George Biro, invented another form of mine in 1938. They observed that the ink used in printing newspapers would dry up quickly and not run. So they invented me so that I would use this ink. As the thick ink that was being used would not flow freely through a nib, Biro built a new type of point. A tiny ball bearing was fitted into the tip. As and when the pen would write on the paper, the ball would automatically roll, thus picking up ink from the cartridge and inscribing it on the paper.

I was actually used as early as 1888 by John J. Loud to mark leather. I proved a great help to the British Royal Air Force in Second World War, as I would not leak at higher altitudes in their fighter planes. Eversharp Co. and Eberhard-Faber in Argentina began to produce me. Milton Reynolds upon visiting Buenos Aires copied my design and started producing me. I was in big demand. Soon, big names like Parker, Sheaffer and Waterman started producing high quality models of me. The ball bearing they used in me was made of tungsten carbide.

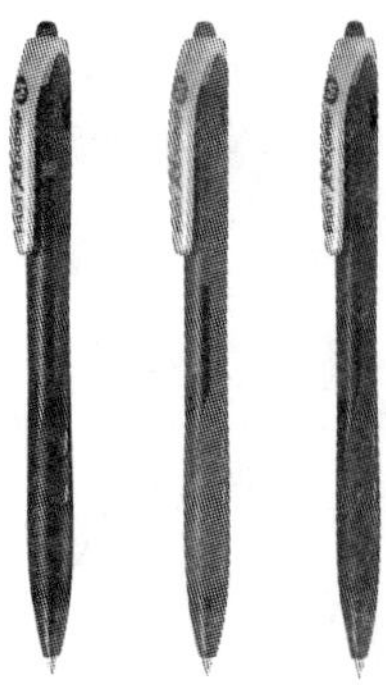

Ink Pen and Ball-point Pen

The fountain pen was invented after using the quill for thousands of years. The invention of the ball-point pen soon followed and it brought a revolution in jotting down all that we wanted without spilling ink.

I am an electronic machine that enables a bank customer to carry out his banking transactions, such as cash withdrawals and checking his account balance at any time. In some cases I allow customers to deposit cash into their accounts, make money transfers and even purchase postage stamps. My first model was produced by NCR in Dundee, Scotland and installed by Barclays Bank.

Don Wetzel, the vice president of product planning at Docutel, along with Tom Barnes and George Chastain registered a patent on me. I was initially used as a cash dispenser. The money would not be directly withdrawn from any account. This later changed. Now, not only do I allow direct cash withdrawal, but also permit customers to withdraw or deposit money from machines that do not belong to their bank. Since I allow withdrawal in local currency, one can conveniently use me when they travel abroad.

Customers are given a plastic card with a magnetic strip that has the customer's account number encoded on it. When they swipe this card and enter a numeric personal identification number, they are able to access their accounts. However, if one enters the number incorrectly several times in a row, I continue to keep the card, thus, ensuring that no unauthorised user gains access to any account. I have a simple data terminal with two input and four output devices. I communicate through a host processor that would be an Internet Service Provider.

I can be made to stand free like a kiosk in a shopping arcade or can be built into a side of a bank or a building. I am of great convenience to people who travel extensively. I may commit a few errors, such as giving out money without debiting the customer's account or even giving out higher value notes than is required. There can also be fake withdrawals. In such a case, the bank has to bear the losses incurred by the customer.

Automatic Teller Machine (ATM)

This is an Automatic Teller Machine. The word 'machine' in the term 'ATM' is certanily redundant, but is widely used. The first ATM was installed in 1969 by Chemical Bank at its branch in Rockville Centre, New York.

Usually I am used for measuring the weight of a person. I am also used in science for deducing the mass of an object. In industrial and commercial applications, I am used to determine the weight of things. I am also sometimes used to measure force as opposed to just the mass. In my 'balance' form, I use the comparison technique in which a beam is used from which a weighing pan and scale pan are suspended.

The object that needs to be weighed is placed on my measuring pan and standard weights are added on my scale pan until my beam is in equilibrium. In my 'spring' form, I use a spring with a known spring constant in which I measure the displacement of my spring in order to deduce the amount of gravitational force applied by the object that is being weighed. This object is usually hung from my spring or placed on a platform. Rack and pinion mechanisms are often used to convert the linear spring motion to a dial reading.

I should be used at a constant temperature or else I may give wrong measurements as my scale gets affected by the weather. For this reason, I am not very popular for commercial applications. I usually give measurements in kilograms or pounds. In some of my other models, I use hydraulic force to measure weight. This force is applied to a piston or diaphragm and transmitted through hydraulic lines to a dial indicator based on a Bourdon tube or electronic sensor.

My most common form of measuring weight electronically is 'force restoration'. In this, I use an electromagnet that pulls against the weight by an appropriate lever or flexure system. The current in the electromagnet is adjusted by a feedback mechanism until a 'null sensor' is centred; at this point the current being fed to the electromagnet is directly proportional to the weight. In my most accurate and expensive electronic form, I offer resolutions of one part in 1,000,000. For this reason, I am rarely used in less expensive systems.

Weighing Scale

This is the weighing scale. Its original form consisted of a beam with a fulcrum at its centre. For highest accuracy the fulcrum would consist of a sharp V-shaped pivot seated in a shallower V-shaped bearing. For high precision, the centre beam balance is the most accurate technology available, especially for calibrating test weights.

The Chinese were experimenting in a lot of explosive devices since 300 BC. They would heat up bamboo to cause an explosion. In the process, a great amount of deliberate experimentation went into developing me. It was observed that a mixture of charcoal, saltpetre and sulphur would result in an explosion if it came in contact with fire. This eventually resulted in their discovery of me. I was developed around 1040.

I was also known as black powder. I was initially used in making fireworks. Later on I was developed for military purposes, such as launching small rockets. During the 13th century, the Chinese were using me in their bombs and cannons. Soon, I was used extensively in wars in the Middle East. I was first used to launch projectiles from a portable gun. This gun was similar in size to the modern rifle in Arabia in 1304. My use in explosives and then in firearms aggravated and evolved the destructive power of weapons.

For about 800 years, I was preferred as an industrial explosive until a more powerful substance was invented. One of my most important chemicals is potassium nitrate. The molecular structure of this chemical, KNO_3, contains three atoms of oxygen, one atom of nitrogen, and one atom of potassium. The three oxygen atoms locked into this molecule provide the 'air' that the fuse and the rocket use to burn the other two ingredients, carbon and sulphur. Thus potassium nitrate oxidises the chemical reaction by easily releasing its oxygen.

The Taoist alchemists brought about the invention of me with the financial support of the Chinese Emperor, Wu Di of the Han dynasty. The alchemist, Wei Boyang, wrote the *Book of the Kinship of the Three* detailing the experiments. I was used to treat skin diseases and as a fumigant to kill insects.

Gunpowder

Gunpowder is a substance which burns very rapidly and is used as a propellant in firearms. As it burns, a subsonic **deflagration** wave is produced.

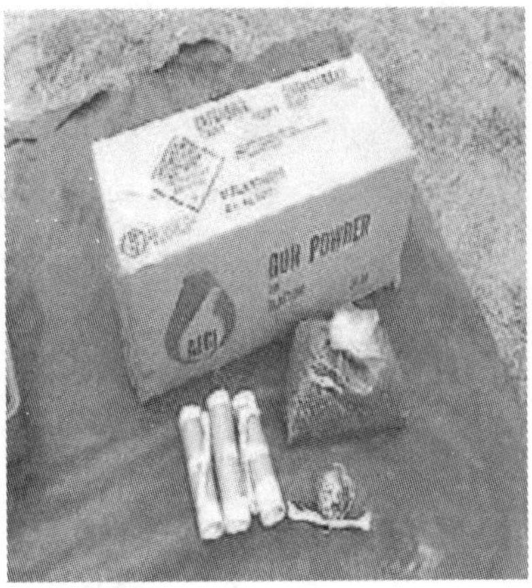

I can be found in a number of places like the car, computer, laptop, cellular phone and many more. I am best described as a can full of chemicals that produces electrons through an electrochemical process. I have two ends, also called terminals: one is positive and the other, negative. The positive terminal is denoted by the '+' sign and the negative terminal by the '–' sign. The electrons remain attracted to the negative terminal.

If a wire is connected between the two terminals, a flow of electrons takes place. Once the wire is connected to a light bulb, or a radio, then I can make them work. I can also keep control on the number of electrons flowing. Since the electrons must flow between the two terminals through a wire for the chemical reaction to take place, I can retain my power by disconnecting the two terminals. Alessandro Volta was the first to develop a workable model of me in 1800 by using zinc, blotting paper soaked in salt-water and silver.

I was called voltaic pile. I became the basis of all my future models by converting chemical energy into electrical energy. Volt is a unit of measurement for measuring electrical potential. Before the electric generator was invented, the Daniel cell was being used to operate telegraphs and door-bells. In 1859, Gaston Plante, a French physicist, developed my lead acid storage form. I would use electrolyte and this made me heavy and difficult to move. This problem was then soon solved with the advent of the dry cell form of mine.

The electrolyte was in a damp paste form which would not leak and was portable and easy to use. The Daniel cell was also known as the Crowfoot cell because of its shape or gravity cell and wet cell. My newest form is the alkaline storage model. This is the most widely used form and was developed by Thomas Alva Edison in 1914. I am described as alkaline since the **electrolyte** I contain is alkaline in nature and not acidic. Like the dry cell, I am easy to use and portable since the electrolyte is not liquid; it is instead, in a dry damp paste form.

Battery

The alkaline batteries are far superior to the zinc-carbon batteries though the zinc-carbon batteries were used quite extensively once upon a time.

I am a popular doll that was invented by Ruth Handler, the co-founder of Mattel, in 1959. My first appearance was at the American Toy Fair in New York. The motive for creating me was to have a teenage fashion doll. When Ruth Handler noticed that her daughter, along with her friends, would love playing with adult dolls cut out from paper or cardboard instead of playing with baby dolls, she thought of creating a life-like doll.

I was designed similar to Lilli, a doll that was modelled on a character in a popular German comic strip. My doll clothes were made out to be realistic looking. I presented the image of the girl-next-door. Soon, I was a big hit among the girls, who loved the fact that they could buy different models of me. I could be a doctor, a rock star, a businesswoman, a women's World Cup soccer player, an astronaut, a firefighter, a UNICEF volunteer and much more. My greatest asset is the fact that I am versatile and can evolve with the ever-changing society.

At first, the idea of selling me was rejected by Mattel. When they finally did begin selling me, the company hit a new sales record in the first year itself. I have had the most successful product line in the history of the toy industry, such that Mattel had to struggle to keep up with the demand of little girls from all over the world. I am now sold in almost 150 countries. I have also represented 45 different nationalities. My *Freundshcafts* meaning 'friendship model' was introduced to commemorate the tearing down of the Berlin Wall in 1990.

A new software was developed with the help of which girls can design, customise and create their own version of me. I have over 43 pets. Collecting me has become a popular hobby even among the adults everywhere. My collection of clothes consists of big names in the fashion industry like Givenchy, Versace, Dolce & Gabana, Vera Wang and Gucci. In 1961, I was introduced in Europe. My first model wore a black and white striped bathing suit and a ponytail. The ponytail went on to become my signature style while pink is my signature colour.

Barbie Doll

Though the Barbie doll has been criticised for advocating sexism and an unattainable physique, it has nevertheless been a rage among children as well as adults all over the world.

I am a mode of transport. I was called wagonway and was used in Germany as early as 1550. The ancient Greeks thought of building me. They used deep grooves in the ground to move heavy wagons. By the 15th century, Europeans used hand-carts on wooden rails. The primitive form consisted of wooden rails over which horse-drawn wagons moved easily than over dirt roads. Wagonways marked the beginning of me as a mode of transport.

By 1776, iron had replaced wood in the rails and wheels on the carts. Wagonways evolved into tramways and spread throughout Europe. Horses still provided all the pulling power. In 1789, an Englishman, William Jessup designed the first wagons with flanged wheels. The flange was a groove that allowed the wheels to grip better on the rail. The invention of me was critical to the invention of the mode of transport. In 1803, Samuel Homfray decided to fund the development of me as a vehicle to replace the horse-drawn carts on the tramways.

Richard Trevithick (1771-1833) built me. On February 22, 1804, I hauled a load of 10 tonnes of iron, 70 men and five extra wagons for 9 m between the ironworks at Penny-Darron and the town of Merthyr Tydfil in Wales. It took about two hours. In 1821, another Englishman, Julius Griffiths patented a passenger model of me. In September, 1825, the Stockton & Darlington Railroad Company began to use me to carry both goods and passengers on regular schedules, and I was designed by English inventor, George Stephenson.

Stephenson's invention pulled six loaded coal cars and 21 passenger cars with 450 passengers over 9 m in an hour. In America, Colonel John Stevens, in 1826, demonstrated the feasibility of steam locomotion on a circular experimental track in New Jersey. I helped in linking landmasses in other parts of the world. My advent allowed quick movement of large numbers of people and products over large distances. I even increased the speed of communication. There are enough tracks in the world to circle the earth more than 100 times.

Railroad

This is the railway or the railroad. Richard Trevithick's invention is considered the first tramway locomotive. However, it was a road locomotive, designed for a road and not for a railroad. In 1829, George Stephenson perfected a practical steam locomotive in England.

Nicholas Jacques Conté, a French chemist, was the first to develop and patent the process of making me in the form of a writing device in the year 1795. I was made with a mixture of clay and graphite. Graphite was discovered in Borrowdale, near Keswick, England when a tree got accidentally uprooted, exposing me as the black substance. The locals would use this to mark their sheep. It was mistaken for the element lead.

European craftsmen played a big roll in designing me. I was a favourite of the European artists and craftsmen. The Italians came up with the idea of taking a hollow stick of wood and inserting a graphite stick in the hollow. Soon a better technique was developed wherein the graphite stick was inserted between the two wooden halves and the two halves were glued together. In 1662, the Germans tried to make the graphite sticks by using powdered graphite, sulphur and antimony.

Nowadays, oil or molten wax is used to make for smoother writing. There is a scale that defines my level of hardness, blackness and fineness: 'H' denotes hardness, 'B' denotes blackness and 'F', fine point. Soon there was a need for removing the marks I made on paper. Charles de la Condamine, a French scientist and explorer, discovered a new material from South America that would serve this need in Europe. The Indian tribes in South America were using this material to stick feathers to their bodies and for making bouncing balls.

In 1770, Edward Naime, an English scientist, accidentally discovered the use of this material and went on to sell it in Europe. This material, however, would easily perish, just like food. To prevent this from happening, Charles Goodyear discovered the process of vulcanisation, named after the Roman god of fire, Vulcan. This process would make this material longer lasting and useable. In 1844, he then went on to patent this process. This material was popularly called *peaux de negres* in Europe and was quite commonly used.

Pencil and Eraser

The writing device is the pencil and it gets its name from the Latin word *penicillus*, meaning 'little tail'. Pencil also means 'brush' in old English. The pencil-mark removing device is called the eraser.

My first ancestor was designed by Oliver Evans in 1844 to make things more bearable for his yellow fever patients. Even though William Cullen demonstrated the principle involved in manufacturing me at the University of Glasgow in 1748, he did not have any practical purpose in mind. Oliver Evans was thus the first to build me. Jacob Perkins built the first practical version of me in 1834. Perkins' model used ether in a **vapour compression cycle**.

The main principle that was used to make me is that liquids absorb heat while evaporating. The liquid used in me evaporates at an extremely low temperature. Just as it feels cool when water or alcohol evaporates on your skin, if you place the liquid inside me on your skin, it will freeze your skin and is definitely dangerous! A German engineer, Carl von Linden, patented the process of liquefying gas in 1876, which is the main system that was used in me.

I am made up of a compressor, heat-exchanging coiled pipes, expansion valve and a liquid that cools as it evaporates. Many industries use pure ammonia for this purpose, which evaporates at -32° C. The compressor compresses the gas, which raises my pressure and temperature. As the gas cools, it condenses into liquid and flows through the expansion valve. This liquid now moves from high pressure to low pressure, and expands and evaporates back to its natural gaseous form.

While evaporating, it absorbs my heat, making me cold. What I basically do is to slow down the activity of bacteria contained in all food so that food doesn't spoil easily. I do this by keeping the food at a lower temperature. Until 1929, I used ammonia, methyl chloride and sulphur dioxide as the cooling agents, which are actually toxic. Chlorofluorocarbons or CFCs released by me are found to increase the hole in the ozone layer. Today CFC-free versions of me are available.

Refrigerator

An engineer from Maryland, USA, Thomas Moore, coined the term 'refrigerator' in 1800. His 'refrigerator' was a cedar tub, insulated with rabbit fur and filled with ice, surrounding a sheet-metal container for transporting butter to Washington DC.

Candles, torches and oil lamps were being used to light up rooms before I arrived. Thomas Alva Edison invented me in 1879 in America and Sir Joseph Wilson Swan in England. Sir Humphrey Davy conducted a few experiments and discovered that when an electrical arc is placed between two poles, it would produce light. My experimental form was first installed in the Place de la Concorde in Paris. This experiment was followed in Europe and America.

There was a constant struggle to invent a simple and reliable form of me that would be easy to use at home and public places. James Prescott Joule discovered that when an electric current is passed through a resistant conductor, it would emit a white, hot glow. This then could be used as luminous energy and became popular as the Joule effect. The problem of discovering the right conductor was soon undertaken. Care was taken to ensure that there was no presence of oxygen, as it would cause the filament to catch fire.

Sir Joseph Wilson Swan successfully constructed my electric form but he had no clue as to how a vacuum could be maintained inside the bulb. Thomas Alva Edison solved this problem by using a carbon filament on October 21, 1879. After making further improvements in my form, he started marketing me. This particular model lasted for 1500 hours. In 1910, William David Coolidge of the General Electric Company, New York, developed the tungsten filament. This proved to be my best form ever.

I have a very simple structure. I consist of two metal contacts that are attached to the ends of an electrical circuit. The metal contacts are connected by stiff wires that are then attached to a thin metal filament. This arrangement is housed within a glass bulb filled with an inert gas. The electric current flows between the two contacts through the stiff wires. The tungsten filament is designed in a coil form so that it easily fits inside the glass bulb. It could be 2 m long and just one hundredth of an inch thick.

Light Bulb

This is the light bulb. Although there were problems with the early incandescent lighting systems in use for years, Edison's reputation as the world's greatest inventor was firmly established with his invention of the bulb.

I am a means of communication. Probably no means of communication has revolutionised the daily lives of ordinary people more than I have. I am a system which converts sound, specifically the human voice, to electrical impulses of various frequencies and then back to a tone that sounds like the original voice. In 1831, an Englishman, Michael Faraday (1791-1867) proved that vibrations of metal could be converted to electrical impulses.

In 1861, Johann Philip Reis (1834-1874) in Germany built a simple apparatus that changed sound to electricity and back again to sound. A crude device, it was incapable of transmitting most frequencies, and it was never fully developed. A practical device was actually invented independently by Elisha Gray (1835-1910) and Scottish-born Alexander Graham Bell (1847-1922). Both men filed for a patent on their designs at the New York Patent Office on February 14, 1876, with Bell beating Gray by only two hours.

Although Gray had built the first steel diaphram/electromagnet receiver in 1874, he wasn't able to master the design of a workable transmitter until after Bell had. The first fully intelligible message on me was passed on March 6, 1876, when Bell, in one room, called to his assistant in another room, "Come here, Watson, I want you." Watson heard the request through a receiver connected to the transmitter that Bell had designed. The first automatic exchange was patented by Almon Strowger of Kansas City in 1891 and installed in 1892.

Bell's greatest success was achieved on March 10, 1876. It marked the death of the multiple telegraph as well. The communications potential contained in his demonstration of being able to 'talk with electricity' far outweighed anything that simply increasing the capability of a dot-and-dash Morse code system could imply. A legal battle ensued between Elisha Gray and Alexander Graham Bell over the invention of the telephone, which was ultimately won by Bell.

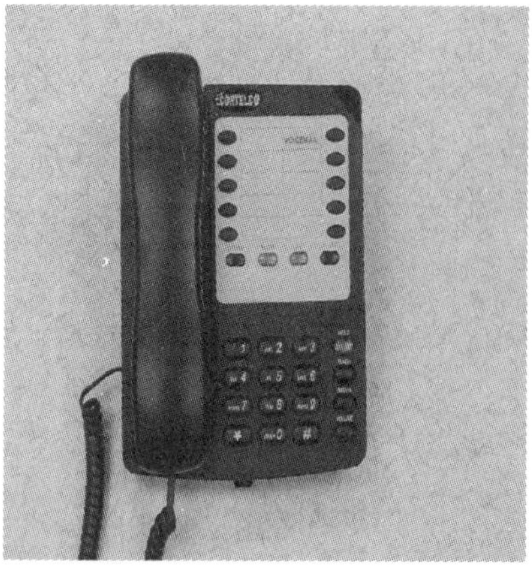

Telephone

This is the telephone. The Bell Telephone Company (later AT&T), the largest in the world, installed the first telephone system, known as an exchange in Hartford, Connecticut in 1877. The first exchange linking two major cities was established between New York and Boston in 1883. The first exchange outside the United States was built in London in 1879.

I am a mode of transport. I am the most revolutionary invention in the history of transportation since the wheel. The basic premise of me is simple: choose a wheeled vehicle from the many types typically pulled by horses or oxen, add a motor and create a self-propelled, personal transportation vehicle. The automobile as we know it was not invented in a single day by a single inventor. My history reflects an evolution that took place worldwide.

The first theoretical plans for building me were drawn up by both Leonardo da Vinci and Isaac Newton. My earliest ancestor was the *Fardier*, a three-wheeled, steam-powered, 2.3-mph vehicle built in 1771 by Nicolas Joseph Cugnot for the French Minister of War. This cumbersome machine was never put into production because it was much slower and harder to operate than a horse-drawn vehicle. It would stop every 10 to 15 min to build up steam power. The steam engine and boiler were separate from the rest of me and were placed in the front.

Amedee Bollee, a Frenchman, built an improved 12-passenger steam vehicle in 1873, but the steam engine proved impractical for a machine that was intended to challenge the speed of a horse-driven buggy. Nicolaus August Otto invented the historically significant gas motor engine in 1876. He built the first practical four-stroke internal combustion engine, which was universally adopted for all my models. The milestone vehicle was built in Germany in 1889 by Gottlieb Daimler and Wilhelm Maybach.

Powered by a 1.5 hp, two-cylinder gasoline engine, I had a four-speed transmission and travelled at 10 mph. Another German, Karl Benz, also built a gasoline-powered model of me the same year. Only a handful of the models were manufactured in Europe and the United States. The first manufacturers in the world who built me for sale were French: Rene Panhard, Emile Levassor (1889) and Armand Peugeot (1891). Ford began producing his Model T in 1908, and by 1927, when this was discontinued, over 18 million had rolled off the assembly line.

Automobile

This is the automobile. The first automobile to be produced in quantity was the 1901 curved Dash oldsmobile, which was built in the United States by Ransom E. Olds. Modern automobile mass production and its use of the modern industrial assembly line is credited to Henry Ford of Detroit, Michigan, who built his first gasoline-powered car in 1896.

I am a mode of communication and entertainment. Earlier devices were based on an 1884 invention called the scanning disc, patented by Paul Nipkow. Riddled with holes, the large disc spun in front of an object while a photoelectric cell recorded changes in light. Depending on the electricity transmitted by the photoelectric cell, an array of light bulbs would glow or remain dark. Nipkow's mechanical system could not scan and deliver a clear, live-action image.

In 1921, the 14-year-old Philo Farnsworth, while mowing hay in rows, realised that an electron beam could scan a picture in horizontal lines, reproducing the image almost instantaneously. At the same time, Russian immigrant, Vladimir Zworykin, had also designed a camera that focused an image through a lens on to an array of photoelectric cells coating the end of a tube. The electrical image formed by the cells would be scanned line-by-line by an electron beam and transmitted to a cathode-ray tube. Farnsworth sought patent for his image dissector in 1927.

In 1934, the British communications company, British Gaumont, bought a licence from Farnsworth to make systems based on his designs. In 1939, the American company RCA did the same. The Second World War interrupted further development of me. In July 1930, the first British play, *The Man with the Flower in his Mouth* was transmitted. In 1936, the British Broadcasting Corporation adopted my service using the electronic technology of Marconi-EMI (the world's first regular high resolution service: 405 lines per picture).

In France, a transmitter was installed on top of the Eiffel Tower in 1935 to transmit signals for me. The RCA fixed another on top of New York's Empire State Building in 1936. John Baird was the first to develop my model that would transmit images in colour. I became commercially feasible in the 1960s.
I carried three tubes for the colours red, blue and green. Japan's Sony Corporation made further improvements in me by combining all the colours in one single tube. This resulted in better colour images and better viewing.

Television

This is the television. John Logie Baird is the inventor of the mechanical television system. He created the first televised pictures of objects in motion (1924), and in 1928 came the trans-Atlantic transmission of the image of a human. Colour television (1928), stereoscopic television and television by infra-red light were demonstrated by Baird before 1930.

I am a means of thrusting a projectile or vehicle forward with the help of a fuel that is burnt in a combustion chamber. This fuel is then released from a nozzle in the rear of the object being propelled. I carry my own oxygen. On the other hand, jet engines take in oxygen from the surrounding air. Jets are far more easily controllable. However, I move faster. I also have the ability to operate in an airless environment like the outer space.

Based on the different types of fuels I use, I can be of two types: solid and liquid. The Chinese first used me in my solid fuel form as fireworks and weapons, around 1232. After being further developed by William Congreve, I was used by the British navy to bombard targets in Napoleonic wars and the war of 1812. He added launching tubes to improve my efficiency and accuracy. Robert H. Goddard first used me in my liquid fuel form on March 26, 1926. By the late 1930s the idea of using me to travel in outer space was greatly speculated.

Wernher von Braun developed my first large and long-range form and I was named V-2 (A-4) missile. During the Second World War, the Germans started building me to fight the British, from a long range. Wernher was always fascinated by space travel and in fact, after the World War, he migrated to the United States to join the American space programme. Also, many of his fellow workers migrated to the then USSR to work in the Soviet space programme. This brought about my major development in both the countries well into the 1960s and 1970s.

My largest form ever to have been built was called Saturn 5. It was 363 ft tall and was capable of delivering 4 million kg of thrust. This particular model was widely used between 1969 and 1972 for sending American astronauts to the moon. It was last used in 1973 to assist in launching the Skylab space station. Today, my largest vehicle form is the Space shuttle. It combines the use of liquid and more affordable solid fuel so as to help me deliver a 3.4 million kg thrust.

Rocket

This is the rocket. The first rocket-powered aircraft was the *Lippisch Ente*, flown in 1928. The only rocket plane ever to be mass produced was the *Messerschmitt Me* 163 in 1944, one of Germany's Second World War attempts at using rocket-powered aircraft.

In my earliest form I was made of a disk that was placed perpendicular to the wind. Judging by the rotation of the disk, one could determine the momentary force of the wind. Dr John T.R. Robinson invented my other form. I consist of four small hollow metallic hemispheres that are mounted one on each end of a pair of horizontal arms, which lie at right angles to each other forming a cross. Passing through the centre of the cross is a vertical axis around which the cups turn.

At any given time a train of wheelwork counts the number of turns that the axis makes and this way, calculates the velocity of the wind. Since the cups are placed symmetrically, the hollow of one cup always faces the wind and at the same time, the back of the cup fixed on the opposite end of the cross also faces the wind. However, the pressure of the wind on this cup is comparatively less. This ensures a continual rotation of the cups. I am favoured for my simplicity.

Calculation of the wind velocity depends largely on the dimensions of the cups as well as the arms. Since the direction of the wind can vary, a wind vane is used so as to let the axis follow the changes. For measuring the pressure of the wind, I can be categorised into two classes — plate and tube. In the former, I have a flat plate that can be either square or circular. While a wind vane ensures that this plate always faces the wind, the pressure of the wind on its face is balanced by a spring.

In the tube class, I have a U-tube that contains liquid with one end bent in a horizontal way, facing the wind. The pressure is calculated by studying the difference in the increased pressure formed in the open mouth of the tube and the decreased pressure formed inside when the wind blows over a ring of small holes in a metallic vertical tube, closed at the upper end. I am used alongside windmills to calculate the wind speed and power generated by the **turbine**.

Anemometer

Leon Battista Alberti, an Italian architect, invented the first mechanical form of the anemometer in 1450. The sonic anemometer can be used to predict the wind speed and direction inside subway tunnels, so as to avoid any mishaps or casualties that can be caused by fire or smoke.

I was invented by a group of physicists that included Dr Donald Keck and Dr Peter Chults. Dr Robert D. Maurier headed this group. In 1970, they finally developed me with an attenuation of only 17 decibels per km. I can be described as a channelled transmission of light through hair-thin glass fibres. This light is prevented from escaping the fibre by total internal reflection.

In this case the fibre core has a higher refractive index than the material around the core, and the light hitting that material is reflected back into the core, where it continues to travel down the fibre. Although I am used widely, my greatest use has been in the field of telecommunications, where I help to transmit audio, video, and data information as coded light pulses. I am becoming the most popular mode of transmitting communications of all kinds, mainly due to my increased carrying capacity. I account for increased bandwidth operation.

Due to this, high-volume and high-speed transfer of information is possible. I can transmit data at the rate of 100M b/s and higher. I am also a low-loss conductor, which is why there is no need for re-amplification of signals in long-distance applications. Since I am a non-metallic conductor, I do not emit or transmit any electromagnetic or radio frequency interferences. I pose no electrical grounding or shorting problems. Even if I get damaged, I do not cause fire or electrical shocks. Thus I am used in mining and petrochemical operations.

I can handle 1,344 two-way voice transmissions on just two strands of fibre. I am used in local area networks, telephones, closed circuit televisions, cable network, for electronic news gathering, military tactical field communication systems and metering. I am coated with multi-layers of plastic in order to absorb shock and provide extra fibre protection. These buffer coatings are available from 250-1,000 microns in either mechanically strippable or chemically strippable form.

Fibre Optics

There are two types of multiple pathway fibres, or multimode fibres: step index and graded index. The discovery of laser technology acted as a catalyst for the development of fibre optics. It is estimated that there are more than 28 million miles of optical waveguided fibres installed throughout the world today.

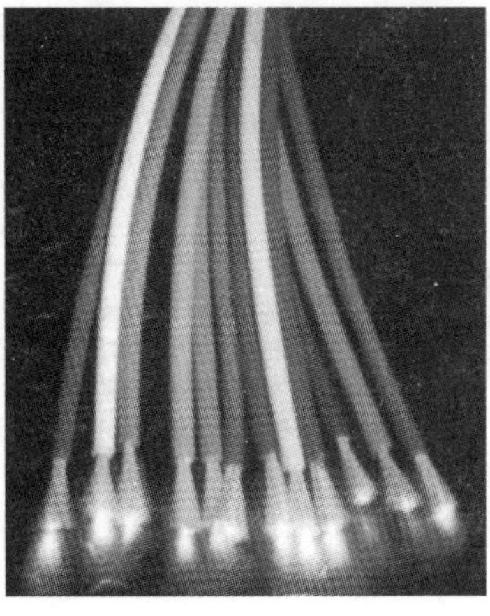

I am a mode of wireless communication. I was first developed in 1879. The first ones were bulky, noisy, and had poor reception. With the advent of improved technologies, such as vacuum tubes and rectifiers, the early device was honed into the interesting little me that became a craze during the 1920s. The first public station for using me opened in Pittsburgh in 1922. I would not have become possible had not the microphone and the audion tube been discovered.

During the second half of the last century, scientists found the identity between light and electromagnetic action that took Guglielmo Marconi to discover me. I can make the electromagnetic waves travel in the air, confined in a conductive media — the ionosphere and the earth surface, and still capable of preserving precisely their own features. During the fall of 1894, Marconi transformed the granary into his laboratory, working among rolls of copper wire, brass spheres, Ruhmkorff coils, Morse keys and electric bells, realising the first elementary sets.

The first weak signals could reach from the window of the granary where the transmitter was placed on the hill to the end of the garden where the receiver was kept. The three points of the letter S travelled in space, reaching the destination. He then took the receiver to the other side of the hill, where Mignani, a farmer, with his gun waited for the ring to sound three times. Marconi pushed three times the key of the transmitter and heard the answer of a distant gunshot: electromagnetic waves had overtaken the obstacle.

It was the month of April 1895. He overcame the difficulties connecting to the oscillator, an antenna and ground, thus obtaining more power. Lee Dee Forest, an American scientist, helped develop the audion tube in 1907. He then later went on to arrange my first ever live broadcast, featuring the world-famous tenor Enrico Caruso from the Metropolitan Opera House in New York on January 13, 1910. My first ever regularly scheduled broadcasting started on November 2, 1920.

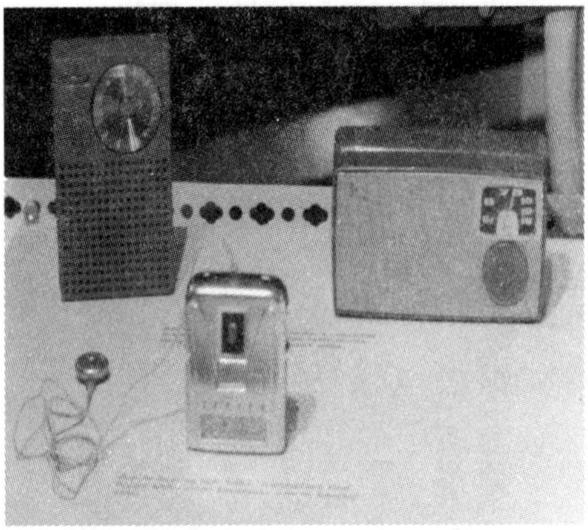

Radio

Radio is a cheap and convenient mode of conveying information and ideas. The first broadcasts consisted primarily of news and world affairs. Later, radios were used to broadcast everything from concerts and sermons to 'Red menace' ideas. On December 10, 1909 Guglielmo Marconi was awarded the Nobel Prize in physics for discovering me.

I am an invention which became a medical breakthrough brought about by Robert Jarvik. In his teen years, he invented an automatic surgical stapler and designed several surgical tools. He became interested in medicine when his father had to go in for an open heart surgery. He designed a device called Jarvik-7. William J. Kolff helped him with his design. I am the first of my kind to be permanent.

Even though his invention was meant to save lives, many people were physically harmed. I was made of dacron, polyester, plastic and aluminum. The Jarvik-7 had an internal power system that energises and regulates the pump through a system of compressed air hoses that enter me through the chest. The air tubes are connected to the chambers and the power system drives the pumps to pump the blood. It was for temporary use because my system was open to infection and many patients fell sick.

Patients had to be kept on blood thinners to prevent clots. The Jarvik-7 model of me was tested on cows and other animals. I was meant to beat at least 1,00,000 times a day. Robert Jarvik soon got permission to implant at least 10 of my type of devices. Dr William Devries was the first surgeon to implant me.

Dr Devries fixed me into a patient named Barney Clark. Since Clark was not approved for a regular heart transplant for various medical reasons, he became a prime candidate for the Jarvik-7. He lived for 112 days. Many developments have been made on the Jarvik-7 model of me so that I can run on a small battery that can be worn and does not need any major operation is being developed now. Maybe some day I will permanently replace the real heart for survival of the patient.

Artificial Heart

This is the artificial heart. The first patient, Barney Clark had to be kept on blood thinners to prevent clots and strokes. He suffered from them anyway and bubbles appeared in his lungs. He finally died from multiple organs failure. Yet Jarvik-7 was still beating. In 1983, Robert Jarvik made the first permanent heart and it helped cardiac patients live longer while waiting for donor hearts.

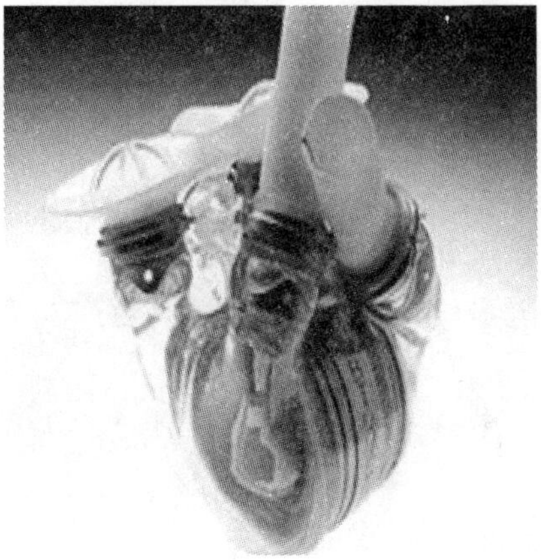

I am a very popular toy all over the world. Theodore Roosevelt, former President of the United States, was responsible for giving me the name. On November 14, 1902, Roosevelt was helping settle a border dispute between Mississippi and Louisiana. During his spare time he attended a bear hunt in Mississippi. During the hunt, Roosevelt came upon a wounded animal of my kind and ordered mercy killing of it.

The Washington Post ran an editorial cartoon by political cartoonist Clifford K. Berryman. Called 'Drawing the Line in Mississippi', the cartoon depicted both state-line dispute and the bear hunt. At first Berryman drew me as a fierce animal; later, he redrew me to make me a cuddly cub. The cartoon and the story it told became popular and within a year, the cartoon became a toy for children.

Morris Michtom made the first official version of me as a toy. He sent Roosevelt a toy and asked permission to use his name for the toy. Roosevelt said yes. Michtom began to mass-produce me. I am a child's toy, usually stuffed with soft material and covered with fur-like material.

Almost at the same time in Germany, Richard Steiff went to the Stuttgart zoo in search of an idea for a new toy. He saw a troupe of performing animals and envisioned a toy like them. Richard sketched me and gave the drawings to his aunt, Margarete Steiff, a renowned toy maker and designer. Margarete took her nephew's drawings and designed a jointed toy model of me based on them.

Teddy Bear

This is the Teddy bear. The new jointed bear appeared for the first time at the Leipzig Toy Fair in 1903. While Richard was packing up his stand at the end of the Fair, an American buyer approached him, and upon seeing the bear, immediately ordered several thousands. This was the beginning of Steiff's Teddy bears we now all know and love.

I refer to the transmission over satellite of programmes directly into the small receiving antennas located at viewers' homes. The transmission is usually done in Ku-band to receiving dishes that can be as small as 45 cm. Stanford University Professor Emeritus, H. Taylor Howard, invented me. He was a leading scientist on several interplanetary NASA probes along with key communication systems on the Apollo programme.

I account for a higher number of subscribers since I help eliminate the cable service provider system in the distribution chain. Thus there is no under-reporting of subscribers as is prevalent in the current cable system. I offer premium quality service that is much better as compared to the ordinary cable network. I also help cut down costs in remote areas where the cable network is expensive. I bring respite to smaller channels as my digital technology allows a provider to compress between eight and 10 channels on a single **transponder**.

For this reason, most big broadcasters are likely to be left with plenty of unutilised transponder space. I am very popular in Europe. I am used by almost 80 per cent of the entire satellite television subscribers. I was launched in the US in 1994. Now there are nearly 13 million subscribers. I also provide value added services like pay per view, video on demand and internet on television. In the Asia-Pacific region, over 2 million people use me. In India I am expensive to operate, for both the consumer and the provider.

Cable companies are given high regard despite the fact that they are not providing the same kind of services that are offered by their international counterparts. Also, foreign investors have reposed faith in the Indian cable companies. There is speculation about the fact that maybe I could have been more successful in India had I been developed before the cable system came about. I pose as a premium product. My demand is greater by up-market viewers.

DTH

The Direct To Home or DTH investments in India are hard to foresee. The reason being the tough regulations set by the government. Such is the fact that the provider or broadcaster can hold only 20 per cent in the venture and foreign investments can be made only up to 49 per cent.

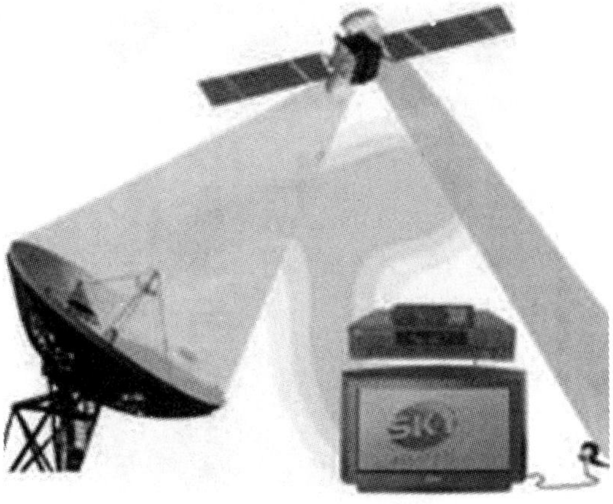

I am a scientific instrument which is used in astronomy to observe the stars. Phoenicians, cooking on sand, discovered glass around 3500 BC, but it took about 5,000 years more for glass to be shaped into a lens for the first type of me. A spectacle-maker probably assembled my first ancestor. Hans Lippershey (*c.* 1570-1619) of Holland is often credited with inventing me, but he almost certainly was not the first to make me.

I was introduced to astronomy in 1609 by the great Italian scientist, Galileo Galilei. Galileo's instrument was similar to a pair of opera glasses which used an arrangement of glass lenses to magnify objects. In 1704, Sir Isaac Newton announced a new concept in my design. Instead of glass lenses, a curved mirror was used to gather in light and reflect it back to a point of focus. This arrangement provided limited magnification — up to 30 times for Galileo — and a narrow field of view: Galileo could see no more than a quarter of the moon's face.

In 1704, Sir Isaac Newton announced a new concept in the instrument's design whereby, instead of glass lenses, a curved mirror was used to gather in light and reflect it back to a point of focus. The reflector instrument that Newton designed opened the door to magnifying objects millions of times — far beyond what could ever be obtained with a lens. Newton's fundamental principle of using a single curved mirror to gather in light remained the same.

In my radio version, I have focused radio antennas in the shape of large dishes constructed of wire meshes, whose openings are smaller than a wavelength. I am often used in pairs or in large groups so as to have large virtual apertures. Currently my record is many times the width of the earth. I also use **optical interferometers** to reflect the X-rays and gamma rays since they penetrate through most metals and glasses. Earlier, the detector in me was the human eye, now it is the charge-coupled device with perfect sensitivity and resolution.

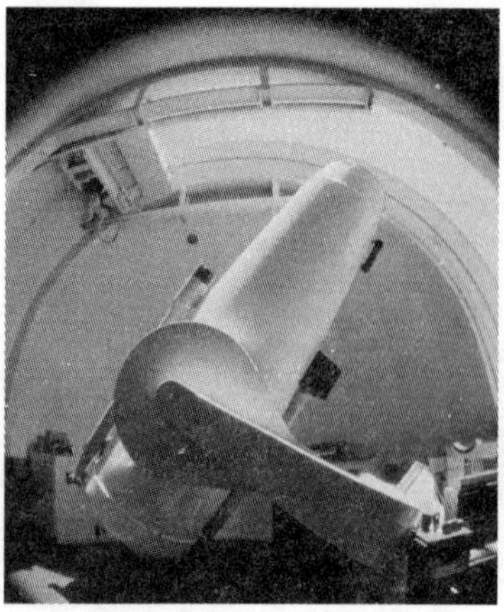

Telescope

This is the telescope. A binocular is an optical instrument for providing a magnified view of distant objects and consists of two similar telescopes, one for each eye, mounted on a single frame. The first binocular telescope was invented by J.P. Lemiere in 1825. Scottish instrument maker, James Short, in 1740 invented the first perfect parabolic and elliptic, distortionless mirror ideal for reflecting telescopes.

I am a business tool. Before the computer, I may have been the most significant everyday business tool. Sholes was a US mechanical engineer who, along with Carlos Glidden and Samual W. Soule, invented the first practical modern machine, patented in 1868 and manufactured by Remington Arms Company in 1873. The type-bar system and the universal keyboard were my novelty, but the keys jammed easily.

To solve the jamming problem, another business associate, James Densmore, suggested splitting up keys for letters commonly used together to slow down typing. This has become today's standard QWERTY keyboard. Sholes lacked the patience required to market me, a new product, and sold the rights to Densmore. He, in turn, convinced Philo Remington (of rifle fame) to market me.

The first sample of me called 'Sholes & Glidden' machine was offered for sale in 1874 but was not an instant success. A few years later, improvements made by Remington engineers gave me market appeal and my sales skyrocketed. The first American patent for me was granted in 1829 to William Austin Burt from Detroit. In 1714, by the grace of Queen Anne, a patent was granted to the English engineer Henry Mill. The invention of at least 112 machines of my type preceded the successful Remington machine.

In 1874, my first commercial model, the Remington Model 1, was put up for sale. Thomas Alva Edison built my first electronic version in 1872. I was used widely only around 1950. I was further developed into one with an electronic memory, so that I could store text, in 1978. The Olivetti Company in Italy and the Casio Company in Japan started producing me simultaneously. My first electric version was called the Blickensderfer. In 1944, IBM designed one version of me wherein I had proportional spacing.

Typewriter

Typewriter is an instrument for producing by manual operation characters similar to those of printing. Corresponding to each key on the instrument's keyboard is a steel type. It is activated through a series of levels or an electronic impulse when its key is pressed.

I am a machine that joins materials. In 1834, Walter Hunt built America's first of my type, which was also the first eye-pointed needle machine. He later lost interest in patenting his machine, because he believed the invention would cause unemployment. I was later re-invented by Elias Howe of Spencer, and patented by Howe in 1846. He patented the lock-stitch version of me. In 1849, Benjamin Wilson introduced an automatic feeding system.

A curved-eye-pointed needle was used in me that passed the thread through the fabric in an arc motion. On the other side of the fabric, a loop was created and a second thread carried by a shuttle running back and forth on a track passed through the loop creating a lockstitch. Howe's design was copied by Isaac Singer and others, leading to extensive patent litigation. Singer's model of me was somewhat different — my needle moved up and down, rather than sideways, and I was powered by a treadle rather than a hand crank.

Isaac Singer patented his concept of the rigid arm for holding the needle and a vertical bar to hold the cloth down against the upward stroke of the needle. Before this, I was used for industrial purposes. However, I used the same lockstitch process and a similar needle. The English inventor and cabinet maker, Thomas Saint was issued the first patent for a complete machine in 1790. The patent describes an awl that punched a hole in leather and passed a needle through the hole.

A later reproduction of Saint's invention based on his patent drawings did not work. Helen Augusta Blanchard of Portland (1840-1922) patented the first zig-zag stitch machine in 1873 and 28 other inventions including a hat-sewing model of me, surgical needles, and other improvements of me. With my advent, I made mass production of clothing on a huge scale possible. This ordinarily would not have been possible with hand stitching.

Sewing Machine

This is the sewing machine invented by the French tailor, Barthelemy Thimonnier, in 1830. Thimonnier's machine used only one thread and a hooked needle that made the same chain stitch which is used in embroidery. The inventor was almost killed by an enraged group of French tailors because they feared unemployment due to this new invention.

I am a method of recording images by the action of light, or related radiation, on a sensitive material. My name is derived from the Greek words *photos* (light) and *graphein* (to draw). My name was first used by scientist Sir John F.W. Herschel in 1839. Louis-Jacques-Mandé Daguerre was the inventor of the first practical process. A professional scene painter for the opera, Daguerre began experimenting with the effects of light upon translucent paintings in the 1820s.

In 1829, he formed a partnership with Joseph Nicéphore Niépce to improve the process Niépce had developed to take the first output in 1826-1827. After years of experimentation, Daguerre developed the daguerreotype. In 1839, he and Niépce's son sold the rights for the daguerreotype to the French government and published a booklet describing the process. The daguerreotype gained popularity quickly; by 1850, there were over 70 daguerreotype studios in New York City.

Daguerréotypes were metal sheets upon which a positive silver image was affixed. This method advanced considerably when sensitised materials could be coated on a glass plate. The first glass negatives were wet plate. They had to be developed quickly before the emulsion dried. The inventor of the first process in me which used a negative from which multiple prints were made was William Henry Fox Talbot, a contemporary of Daguerre.

Talbot had been experimenting with silver iodide and silver nitrate-coated papers, in which negative images were fixed on paper. Many positive contact prints could be made from these negatives. In 1889, George Eastman, realising the potential of the mass market, used a newly invented film with a base that was flexible, unbreakable and could be rolled. Emulsions coated on a cellulose nitrate film base, such as Eastman's, made the mass production of me a reality.

Photography

This is photography. In the early 1940s, commercially viable colour films (except Kodachrome, introduced in 1935) were brought to the market. These films used the modern technology of dye-coupled colours in which a chemical process connects the three dye layers together to create an apparent colour image.

The Taj Mahal — a photographer's delight.

I am made from cocoa beans. During 1500-400 BC, the Olmec Indians were the first to grow cocoa beans as a domestic crop. Initially the consumption of cocoa beans was restricted to the Mayan society's elite, in the form of an unsweetened drink made from the ground beans. In AD 600, the Mayans migrated to northern regions of South America, establishing the earliest known cocoa plantations in Yucatan.

During the 14th century, I became popular as a drink among the Aztec upper classes who usurped me from the Mayans and were the first to tax the beans. The Aztecs called me *xocalatl*, meaning warm or bitter liquid. In 1544, some Dominican friars took a delegation of Kekchi Mayan nobles to visit Prince Philip of Spain. The Mayans brought gift jars of beaten cocoa, mixed and ready to drink. Spain and Portugal did not export the beloved drink to the rest of Europe for nearly a century.

In the 16th-century Europe, cocoa gained popularity as a medicine and **aphrodisiac**. In 1657, the first shop, called the The Coffee Mill and Tobacco Roll was opened in London by a Frenchman. Costing 10-15 shillings per pound, I was considered a beverage for the elite class. Eating me in a solid form was introduced in the form of rolls and cakes, served in emporiums which sold my products. In 1753, Swedish naturalist, Carolus Linnaeus renamed me *theobroma*, the Greek word for 'food of the gods'.

In 1765, I was introduced to the United States when Irish maker of me, John Hanan with American Dr James Baker built America's first chocolate mill and by 1780, began to make the famous BAKER'S product. Recent studies claim that I carry high levels of chemicals known as phenolics, some of which may help lower the risk of heart disease. I contain about 300 known chemicals, including caffeine. Theobromine, a mild stimulant, is also found. All these stimulants increase the activity of **neurotransmitters** (brain chemicals) in parts of the brain that control man's ability to pay attention and stay alert.

Chocolate

This is chocolate. In 1819, the pioneer of Swiss chocolates, François Louis Callier, opened the first Swiss chocolate factory. In 1847 Joseph Fry & Son discovered a way to mix some of the cocoa butter back into the 'dutched' (smoother consistency) chocolate, and added sugar, creating a paste that could be moulded. The result was the first modern bar. In 1868, John Cadbury mass marketed the first boxes of chocolate candies.

I am a device with which one can measure the water vapour, moisture content of air or any gas for that matter. In other words, I indicate the level of humidity. My most popular form is the 'dry and wet bulb psychrometer'. As the name suggests, I have two thermometers usually containing mercury. One has a wet base and the other, a dry base. As the temperature increases, the water content of the constant wet bulb evaporates and there is a fall in the thermometer reading.

After consulting a calculation table and comparing the readings of both the thermometers, the relative humidity can be calculated. My 'Sling' form measures the humidity in a moving air stream, whereas my 'Screen' form measures the wet bulb temperature in still air. Horace Bénédict de Saussure, a Swiss physicist, invented the other type of me that used an organic substance like human or animal hair to measure relative humidity in 1783. It is gauged by the amount of contraction or expansion of the hair due to the moisture content.

There is yet another form of mine: 'Dew Point' that measures humidity by the condensation of moisture on a mirror exposed to open air. I am most sought after by airconditioning engineers. I can also measure humidity by measuring the electrical resistance created by semiconductors, such as a thin piece of lithium chloride. My first crude form was developed by Leonardo da Vinci. Francesco Folli developed my practical form in 1664. Robert Hooke made an improvement in my form.

In order to see changes that occur over time, many (forms of me) record the value of humidity on a piece of graduated paper so that the values can be read off the chart. However, modern instruments often use electronic means of recording the information.

Hygrometer

Robert Hooke improved upon the hygrometer. In 1820, British chemist and meteorologist, John Frederic invented a dew-point hygrometer, which is now in widespread use.

I am a game of words where the player is given a hint and the player then fills in the number of letters, in a grid of boxes by finding the right words. British-born journalist, Arthur Wynne, invented me in 1913. Arthur Wynne (who migrated to the United States) wrote my first game for an American newspaper called the *New York World*. This first game was published on December 21, 1913, in the shape of a diamond.

Some say that the first form of me, intended primarily for children, appeared in England in the 19th century. In the US, I developed into a popular adult pastime. Wynne based his game on a similar, much older, game played in ancient Pompeii, calling it 'magic squares' or 'word squares'. In 1997, the patent for this game was awarded to Variety Games Inc. The first computer software programme patented me.

In 1930, the *London Times* printed their first sample of me. *New York Times* set the standards for my professional versions, for example, symmetrical grids with answers at least three-letters long. In time, I became subtler. I would include pun-based clues, multiple-word answers, and overarching themes.

At first only the *New York World* carried me as a weekly feature. But in 1924, Simon and Schuster published the first collection of me in book form. These days I can be found in every major alphabet-based language, all over the world including the internet. In the US, there are annual tournaments that draw experts from every walk of life. Arthur Wynne's 'mental exercise' has become a national and international institution.

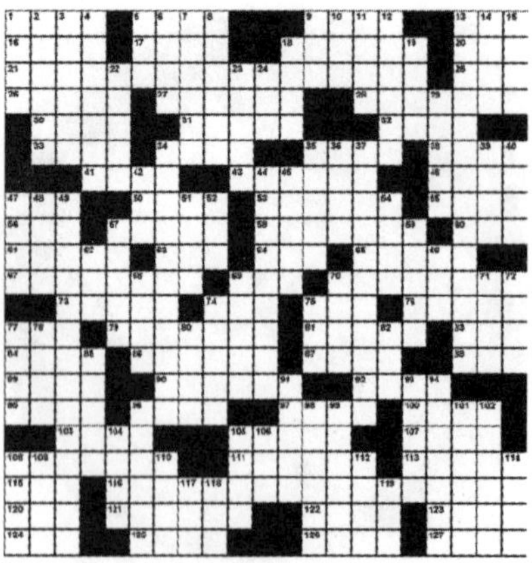

Crossword Puzzle

This is the crossword puzzle. The name of the first crossword puzzle was later switched to 'cross-word' and then to 'crossword'. The crossword is the most common variety of a word puzzle in the world.

I am one of the most popular carbonated drinks. I was invented in May 1886 by Dr John Pemberton, a pharmacist from Atlanta, Georgia, who concocted the formula in a three-legged brass kettle in his backyard. I was given my name by book-keeper Frank Robinson, who first scripted the name for me into the flowing letters which has become the famous logo of today. I was first sold to the public at the soda fountain in Jacob's Pharmacy in Atlanta on May 8, 1886.

Until 1905, I was marketed as a tonic and contained extracts of cocaine as well as the caffeine-rich kola nut. By the late 1890s, I became America's most popular fountain drink. With another Atlanta pharmacist, Asa Griggs Candler, at the helm, the company increased its sales by over 4,000 per cent between 1890 and 1900. By the turn of the century, I was sold across the United States and Canada. Around the same time, the company began selling me in syrup form through independent bottling companies licenced to sell me.

I was consumed far and wide but my first international push came in the 50s and 60s. I took American tourists by surprise when they discovered that I would cost the same as a glass of brandy. I probably helped in popularising America around the world. As Candler hit upon the idea of carbonating me, the bubbles made a huge difference. It was as though they struck gold. He figured that he had to just get the people to try me and that I would soon be everyone's favourite.

Even today, the US soft drink industry is organised on this principle. I was initially sold as a patent medicine for five cents a glass at soda fountains, which were popular in America at the time, thanks to a belief that carbonated water was good for health. By 1888, my three versions sold by three separate businessmen were on the market.

Coca Cola

This is Coca Cola. On April 23, 1985, the trade secret 'new coke' formula was released. Today, products of the Coca Cola company are consumed at the rate of more than one billion drinks per day. Contrary to popular belief, Coca Cola never contained **cocaine.**

I am a whirlpool bath in a tub fitted with pipes, an electric pump and water jets. The pump circulates the water through the pipes using an underwater suction fitting and several underwater jets. Each jet contains a **venturi** — a vented constriction near its opening that injects air into the water. In most cases, the ratio of air to water can be adjusted with a central control at each jet on both sides.

In 1968, Roy Jacuzzi invented and marketed the first type of me by incorporating jets into the sides of the tub. The Jacuzzi brothers introduced me at California's Orange County Fair. In addition to the first patent, the Jacuzzi Company has 250 worldwide patents for advancements in pump systems, jet technology, air controls and product design. The history of the Jacuzzi company began in the early 1900s when the Jacuzzi brothers immigrated to California from Italy.

Working together, they made strides in aviation by inventing the first enclosed cabin monoplane. I first helped in the progress of the agricultural pump industry. Later on, I went on to become a popular fixture in almost every American house. I was used to treat patients suffering from arthritis. I paved the way for invention of the first whirlpool bath. I am commonly found in luxury hotels and on board cruise ships. I can help people to relax.

I have been blamed for accidentally spreading diseases. Since I allow the emulsion of oxygen into water, I naturally oxygenate the skin tissue. This accounts for a general feeling of well-being. I am marketed through brand names including Jacuzzi, Sundance, Eljer, Zurn, Wilkins and Rainbow.

Jacuzzi

The whirlpool bath is called the **jacuzzi**, named after the inventor. The inventor brothers later made great advancements in the agricultural pump industry and, of course, in the whirlpool bath industry.

I am a device with which it is possible to jump from a height without getting hurt. Credit for my invention goes to Sebastien Lenormand who demonstrated my principle in 1783. However, I and other devices had been imagined and sketched by Leonardo da Vinci (1452-1519) centuries earlier. Fellow Italian Fauste Veranzio, who constructed a device based on da Vinci's drawing, jumped down from a Venice tower in 1617.

Jean Pierre Blanchard (1753-1809), a Frenchman was probably the first person to actually use such a device in an emergency. In 1785, he dropped a dog in a basket to which I was attached, from a balloon high in the air. In 1793, Blanchard claims to have escaped from an exploded hot air balloon with my help. Blanchard also developed the first such foldable me, made from silk. Uptil that point I was made from rigid frames. In 1797, Andrew Garnerin was the first person recorded to jump using me without a rigid frame.

I am an umbrella-like device designed to retard the descent of a falling body by creating drag as I pass through the air. My special qualities are that I permit slow descent from a height, that I am highly stable, have little weight, a small area, and retain my shape and maintain balance in descent. Garnerin also designed the first air vent in me, intended to reduce oscillations. Grant Morton and Captain Albert Berry jumped from an airplane in 1911 with me worn on their backs. In 1914, Georgia 'Tiny' Broadwick made the first free fall jump.

I am used by paratroopers to enter enemy territory. Smoke-jumpers and firefighters also use me to enter remote areas to build firebreaks. Sometimes I am used with bombs, like the 'daisy cutters' and the 'cluster bombs'. I am fitted on to ejector seats of jet fighters. I am specially designed to open softly for skydivers. This way, I rarely create strap bruises from the opening shock. My powered form is like the ultralight aircraft.

Parachute

This is the parachute. The word 'parachute' is said to have come into being by putting together the prefix *para* and the noun *chute*. The idea of parachutes for military personnel was first suggested by late Col. William (Billy) Mitchell, during the First World War, even before they had chutes for American flyers.

My companions and I are electromagnetic waves of short wavelength, capable of penetrating a particular thickness of matter. Our electromagnetic nature became evident when it was found that crystals bend their path in the same way as gratings bend visible light. The orderly rows of atoms in the crystal acted like the grooves of a grating.

In 1895, Wilhelm Conrad Röntgen accidentally discovered an image cast from his cathode ray generator, projected far beyond the possible range of the cathode rays. Further investigation showed that we were generated at the point of contact of the cathode ray beam on the interior of the vacuum tube, that we were not deflected by magnetic fields, and that we penetrated many kinds of matter.

A week after his discovery, Röntgen took a photograph of his wife's hand by using us, which clearly revealed her wedding ring and her bones. The photograph electrified the general public and aroused great scientific interest in the new form of radiation. Röntgen was the one to name me, the new form of radiation. The images produced by me are due to the different absorption rates of different tissues.

Calcium in bones absorbs us the most, so bones look white on a film recording of the image. Fat and other soft tissues absorb less, and look grey. Air absorbs the least, so lungs look black on a **radiograph**. Letting a stream of fast electrons come to a sudden stop at a metal plate produces me. Studies say that when the sun or the stars emit me, then too I am produced from fast **electrons**.

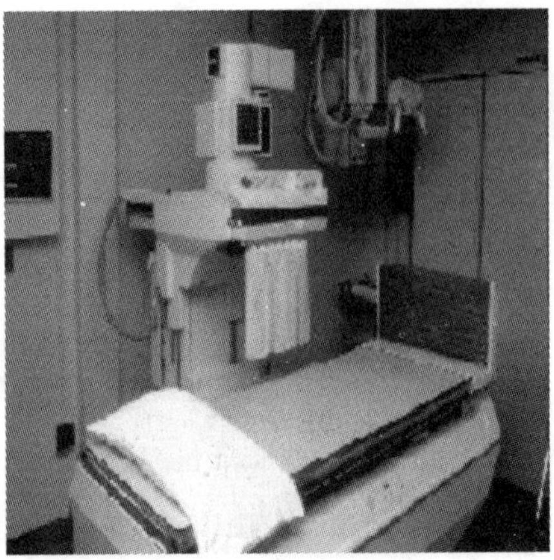

X-ray

These rays are X-rays. Medical X-rays are produced by letting a stream of fast electrons come to a sudden stop at a metal plate. Thus X-ray is a type of radiation that can go through many solid substances, allowing hidden objects such as bones and organs in the body to be photographed.

I am a copying process based on electrostatic energy. In 1937, I was invented by an American law student, Chester Carlson, and I became commercially available in 1950, marketed by the Xerox Corporation. I derive my name from the Greek word for 'dry writing'. Carlson was frustrated with the slow mimeograph machine and the cost of photography. It led him to invent a new way of copying, and this electrostatic process helps reproduce words on a page in a few minutes.

Carlson had a hard time finding investors in his new invention. He was turned down by IBM and the US Army Signal Corps; it took him eight years to find an investor. The Haloid Company, which later became a corporation, agreed to invest in mass production of me. Chester Carlson was both a research engineer and a patent attorney. He filed a patent application in April 1939. I am now widely used in office as a copying machine.

Though I was introduced to the world after the advent of the typewriter in 1867 and before the invention of the fax machine, I brought about a revolution in business and industrial workplaces. My name was formed from the Greek word *xeros*, meaning 'dry'. Before Chester Floyd Carlson invented me with his thorough research and study, the Hungarian scientist, Paul Selenyi, first put the basic theory forward.

Carlson developed me in such a way so that I would use heat, light and electricity to print a dry powdered pigment on to paper. I was first used in an office to make copies on ordinary paper and was introduced in 1959. I would produce seven copies within a minute. Slowly and steadily, due to my efficiency and utility, I was in great demand and I still continue to be a basic necessity in almost every office the world over.

Xerox

The process is xerography. Xerox Corporation also trademarked the name 'Xerox' and has protected the name carefully. Xerography was the invention that no one wanted, little realising that one day it would change the world.

I was invented by Harry Brearley of Sheffield, England, in 1871. After studying very hard at a private and night school, he became an expert in analysing me. His father, who worked at a steel smelter would guide him. In 1908, Brearley set up the Brown Firth Laboratories, which was financed by two leading Sheffield steel companies of the day. In 1912, he tried to solve the problems being encountered by a small arms manufacturer.

The internal diameter of their rifle barrels would erode away too quickly because of over-heating and the discharge of gases. Brearley started experimenting with steel containing chromium since it has a higher melting point as compared to other types of steel. His aim was to find a type of steel that would be resistant to erosion. He used the crucible process and then the electric furnace. He would study the grain structure using a microscope. He would then test samples with vinegar and other food acids, such as lemon juice.

Once he discovered my unique ability to be rust free, he thought of revolutionising the cutlery industry since the only type of cutlery in use was made of carbon steel and with silver or nickel plating. He got a few knives made by the local cutler, R.F Mosley. Brearley's form of metal could be supplied in a hardened and tempered form. At the Krupp Iron Works in Germany, Eduard Maurer and Benno Strauss developed another form of me that was more softer, more resistant to acids, ductile and easier to work with.

My production came to a standstill around the time of the First World War. Brearley's successor, Dr W. H Hatfield, developed an even better form of me in 1924 using 18 per cent chromium and 8 per cent nickel. I am now a type of ferrous alloy with a minimum of 10.5 per cent chromium content. The chromium forms a thin layer that is water and air resistant, thus protecting the metal beneath. Also, if this layer is scratched off, it soon reforms. This phenomenon is called passivation. I can be classified by my crystalline structure.

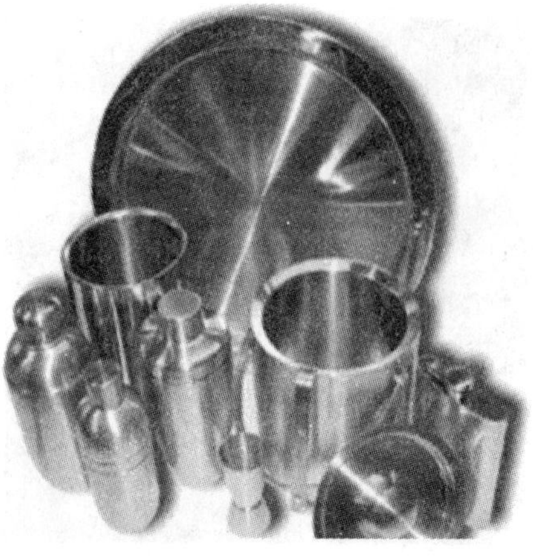

Stainless Steel

The reason for the name stainless steel is the fact that it stains less or rusts less than ordinary steel. It is used for making cutlery, automobile exhausts, razor blades, tools, and nuts and bolts.

I am an organic material derived from cellulose. Once heated, I can be moulded but can retain my shape when cooled. The first such man-made material was unveiled by Alexander Parkes at the 1862 Great International Exhibition in London. The public dubbed it 'the Parkesine'. Parkes claimed that this new material could do anything that rubber was capable of, and that too at a lower price.

He discovered that I was transparent and could be carved into thousands of different shapes. During the latter part of the 19th century, a rush was on to find a replacement for ivory in billiard balls. John Wesley Hyatt, an American, finally came upon the solution in 1866 by discovering celluloid, a form of me. But due to my highly brittle nature, he added camphor — a derivative of the laurel tree.

This addition made me the first thermoplastic: a substance moulded under heat and pressure into a shape it retains even after the heat and pressure are removed. Celluloid was used in the first flexible photographic film for still and motion pictures. Leo Bakeland created a liquid resin which he named Bakelite, another form of me. This new material would not burn, boil, melt, or dissolve in any commonly available acid or solvent.

Cellophane, another modified cellulose and a member of my family, was discovered by Dr Jacques Edwin Brandenberger, a Swiss textile engineer, who came upon the idea for a clear, protective, packaging layer in 1900. Another important innovation of me was polyvinyl chloride (PVC), or vinyl. Waldo Semon, a B.F. Goodrich organic chemist, was attempting to bind rubber to a metal when he stumbled across PVC, which was inexpensive, durable, fire-resistant and easily malleable.

Plastics

This family of organic materials belongs to plastics. Since the 1950s, plastics have been providing improved packaging to giving us new textiles, permitting the production of wondrous new products and cutting-edge technologies in televisions, cars and computers. Polyethylene, teflon, velcro are all part of the plastics family.

I am a prize awarded annually, irrespective of the recipient's nationality, in six areas — peace, literature, physics, chemistry, physiology or medicine, and economic science — to those who, during the preceding year, had conferred the greatest benefit on mankind. I carry with me worldwide recognition that highlights the recipient's life and work and I provide funds to them to continue further with their mission.

I am used to attract the best and the brightest minds, be they students or scholars. Winning me proves a life-changing honour. The laureate may be an internationally known figure (such as Mother Teresa, winner of the 1979 prize) or a scientist picked from obscurity (like Richard R. Ernst, who won the 1991 prize) for refinements in nuclear magnetic resonance spectroscopy.

I was instituted by a Swedish chemist and engineer who invented dynamite, leaving behind $9 million in his will to establish the prizes. He was an industrialist who created a controllable combustible that made blasting rock and the construction of canals and tunnels a relatively safe process. He also contributed to the invention of synthetic rubber, artificial silk and synthetic leather.

He held more than 350 patents. His family members were shocked when they learned that this individual had willed all his wealth to establish the prizes. They contested his will, but his final wishes were executed and the first awards were distributed in 1901, on the fifth anniversary of his death.

Nobel Prize

This is the Nobel Prize. The prize in economics was established in 1968 by Riksbank, the Swedish bank, in honour of its 300th anniversary. Stockholm's Royal Swedish Academy of Sciences administers the award in physics and chemistry, the Royal Caroline Medical Institute in physiology or medicine, and the Swedish Academy oversees the prize in literature. The Norwegian Storting, or Parliament, awards the Nobel Peace prize.

During Second World War, two scientists invented the magnetron — a tube that produces microwaves. Installing magnetrons in Britain's radar system, the microwaves were able to spot Nazi warplanes on their way to bomb the British Isles. The idea of using microwave energy to cook food just happened to occur to Dr Percy LeBaron Spencer of the Raytheon Company when he discovered that radar waves had melted a candy bar in his pocket.

Dr Spencer initially started building me as a metal box with an opening into which he fed microwave power. The energy entering the box was unable to escape, thus creating a higher density electromagnetic field. Food was placed inside me and with the help of microwave energy the food was heated up. After conducting many experiments, he realised that microwave heating could rapidly raise the internal temperature of many foods. He then invented my first form and named me Radar Range.

I was commercially sold in 1954. Since I was large and expensive, only restaurants and big institutions could afford to use me. In 1967, my domestic version came in use in home kitchens. By 1971, my price fell and my capabilities increased. I revolutionised cooking once and for all and laid the foundation of a multimillion-dollar worth business. Microwaves are the shortest radio waves with a length of 0.1 mm and a frequency of 3 x 101 Hz. They are non-ionising in nature and are distributed over a continuous range — the electromagnetic spectrum.

This means that microwaves do not detach charged particles and produce atoms with an unbalanced plus or minus charge. Thus, they can safely produce heat and not cause food to become radioactive. They are also reflected off from most metals. In fact, this brought about the invention of the radar. I was improved and refined and resulted in a more reliable and lightweight cooker that was affordable. I was used in industries to dry potato chips and roast coffee beans and peanuts. I was also used for defrosting, pre-cooking and tempering meat.

Microwave Oven

Microwaves are being used to dry cork, ceramics, paper, leather, tobacco, textiles, pencils, flowers, wet books and match heads. The microwave oven that was once considered a luxury item has now become a necessity in most residential homes and is ideal for cooking meals in the shortest possible time.

I am a writing instrument designed to carry my own supply of ink. Louis Waterman obtained the patent for me in 1884. The oldest type of me that has survived today was designed by a Frenchman named M. Bion in 1702. However, the early versions of me were plagued by ink spills and other failures that left me impractical and hard to sell.

My design came after a thousand years of using quills as writing devices. I am made up of a nib, which comes in contact with the paper; the feed or black part under the nib, to control the ink flow from the reservoir to the nib; and the round barrel that holds the nib and feed on the writing end, protects the ink reservoir internally. My type of writing instruments contain an internal reservoir for ink. The different ways that reservoirs were filled proved a most competitive area in the industry.

The earliest 19th-century model of me used an eyedropper; by 1915, nearly all had switched to self-filling soft and flexible rubber sac as an ink reservoir. The different fillers used over the ages are the button filler, the lever filler, the click filler, the matchstick filler, the coin filler. There are nine standard nib sizes with three different nib-tip cuts: straight, oblique and italic. The early inks caused steel nibs to quickly corrode but gold nibs held up to the corrosion.

Iridium used on the very tip of the nib replaced gold because gold was too soft. Most owners had their initials engraved on the clip. The ink cartridge introduced around 1950 was a disposable, pre-filled plastic or glass cartridge designed for clean and easy insertion.

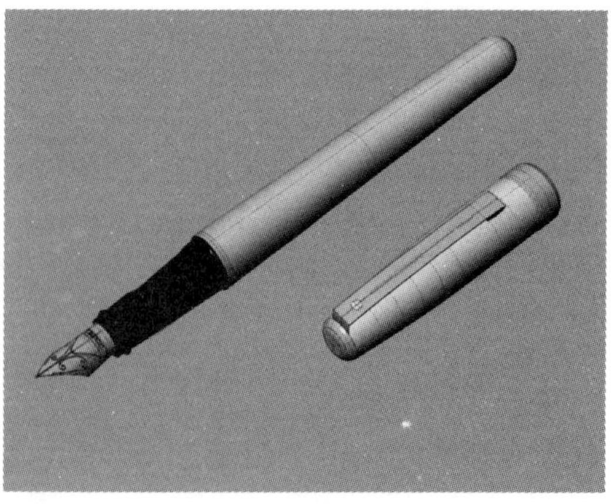

Fountain Pen

This is the fountain pen. It took about four months to break since the nib was designed to flex when pressure was put on it (allowing the writer to vary the width of the writing lines). Each nib wore down according to each owner's own writing style. The introduction of the ballpoints, however, overshadowed the invention of the cartridge and dried up business for the fountain pen industry.

I am an imaginary line which runs from the North Pole to the South Pole. Known as zero longitude, I am the line from which all other lines of longitude are measured, including the line that runs 180° away from Greenwich, also known as the **International Date Line**. In 1884, I was defined by the position of the large 'Transit Circle' telescope in the Greenwich Observatory's Meridian Building.

The transit circle was built by Sir George Biddell Airy, the seventh Astronomer Royal, in 1850. The cross-hairs in the eyepiece of the Transit Circle precisely defined 0° longitude for the world. As the earth's crust is moving very slightly all the time, my exact position is now moving very slightly too, but the original reference for the zero degree longitude of the world remains the Airy Transit Circle in the Royal Observatory.

Since the late 19th century, I have served as the reference line for Greenwich Mean Time. Before this, almost every town in the world kept its own local time. There was no national or international convention which set how time should be measured, or when the day would begin and end, or what length an hour might be. However, with expansion of railway and communication networks during the 1850s and 1860s, the worldwide need for me as a standard became imperative.

The Greenwich Meridian was chosen as the 0° longitude in 1884. Forty-one delegates from 25 nations met in Washington DC for the International Meridian Conference. By the end of the conference, Greenwich had won the prize of 0° longitude by a vote of 22 to 1 against (San Domingo), with two abstentions (France and Brazil).

The Prime Meridian

This is the Prime Meridian. There were two main reasons for choosing Greenwich: firstly that USA had already chosen Greenwich as the basis for its own national time-zone system; second, that in late 19th century, 72 per cent of the world's commerce depended on sea-charts which used Greenwich as the Prime Meridian.

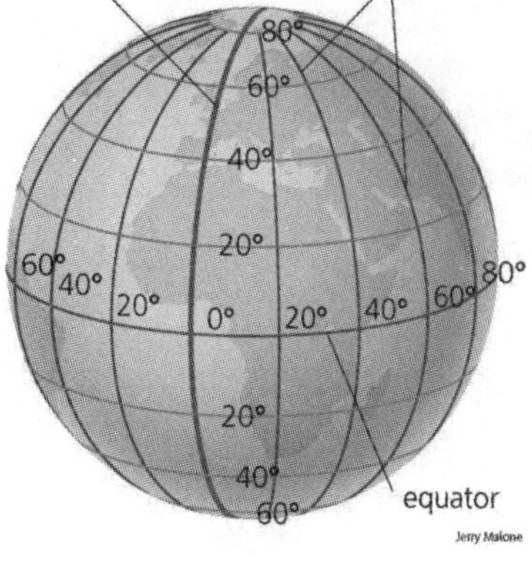

I am a weapons system that delivers explosive warheads to our targets by means of propulsion. My first part describes a jet-propelled missile which is propelled forward from the rearward ejection of matter, like hot gases at a high velocity. The process was developed in China, where firework displays and gunpowder were invented. In 18th century, Hyder Ali, prince of Mysore, developed the first war weapon that used metal cylinders to hold combustion powder for propulsion.

Although the hammered soft iron he used was crude, the strength of the black powder was much higher than the earlier paper construction. In USA, Robert Goddard invented liquid-fuelled weapons and a control mechanism for me. During the First World War, he developed a number of designs of small military weapons to be launched from a lightweight hand launcher; they became the forerunners of the bazooka of the Second World War.

In mid 1940, Clarence N. Hickman, who had worked with Robert Goddard during the First World War, supervised the development of a refined design of a hand launched model of me. The new version, about 50 cm long, 10 cm in diameter and weighing 3.5 pounds, was fired from a steel tube that became popularly known as the **bazooka** used chiefly in attending tanks.

The Germans were in the forefrunt in this category of weapons and their 150 mm and 210 mm weapons were very effective. I was fired from a variety of towed and vehicle-mounted multitube launchers, from launching rails on the sides of armoured personnel carriers, and for massive bombardments from my packing crates.

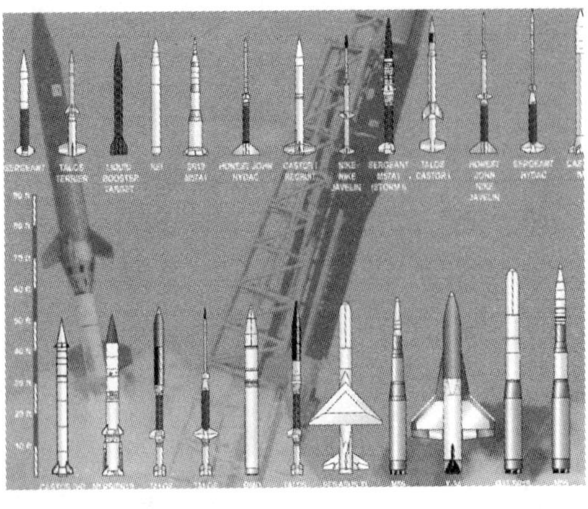

Rocket and Missile System

This is the modern rocket and missile system. The V-2 was a single-stage, fin-stabilised device propelled by liquid oxygen and ethyl alcohol to a maximum range of about 200 m. It was first successfully launched on October 3, 1942, and was fired towards Paris on September 6, 1944.

In earlier times, waste mainly consisted of ash from fires, wood, bones, broken tools and pottery, bodies and vegetable waste. It was usually buried into the ground. These helped form compost and further improve the soil quality. When man evolved from a hunter-gatherer to a farmer and the population increased, the problem of waste disposal soon arose. Nearly 4,000 years ago there is evidence to show that composting was carried out in China as well as Europe.

Vegetable wastes were fed to livestock and green waste was used as fertiliser. Pigs were most often used for disposing of municipal waste. Timber was often salvaged and reused in construction and in building ships. Materials such as gold was melted down and then recasted. With the onset of the Industrial Revolution, scrap metal, paper and non-ferrous metals were recovered. As civilisations grew, societies everywhere started developing better forms of waste disposal. I have many environmental advantages.

I reduced the demand for virgin resources. I also reduced the amount of wasteland filled. However, energy is still used in the process and I cannot completely replace the need for the raw materials. Excessive trash has led to spread of bubonic plague, cholera and typhoid fever to name a few. For this reason, garbage production must be dealt with in a responsible fashion. Toxic and hazardous waste is usually produced by photo developers, metal finishers, gas stations and auto mechanics.

A huge quantity of waste is created in the process of mining and production. For every tonne of post-consumer waste, nearly 20 tonnes of pre-consumer waste is created along the way in the manufacturing process. With my help, waste materials are collected and used again as raw materials for new products. This includes collecting of waste, separation, processing, manufacturing and purchasing items made from such waste. Segregation of waste is very important so that only compatible wastes are disposed of together.

Recycling

In India, recycling has been around for many years. It is undertaken by the informal sector. This sector includes rag pickers, small middlemen, transporters, larger middlemen and finally, reprocessors. Delhi has the biggest recycling base in the country.

I am a form of alternative medicine, stressing on the concept of striking a balance in healing. We can learn to heal ourselves or remain healthy by staying in balance. I am the most holistic or comprehensive medical system, meaning 'the science of life' in Sanskrit. According to my philosophy, the entire cosmos is an interplay of the energies of the five great elements — space, air, fire, water and earth.

I am a science that teaches how to live in a natural balance, confined not only to the proper functioning of the mind, body and soul but to establishing a natural and balanced relationship with Nature as a whole. I include a balanced relationship between man and all the creatures, the climate and the society man lives in.

Knowledge about me originated in India more than 5,000 years ago and is often called the 'mother of all healing'. I stem from ancient Vedic culture and was taught for thousands of years in an oral tradition by accomplished masters to their disciples. Some knowledge of me was set to print a few thousand years ago, but much of it is inaccessible.

I lay great emphasis on prevention and encourage maintaining health by paying close attention to balance in life through right thinking, diet, lifestyle and herbs. According to me, each person has a particular pattern of energy — an individual combination of physical, mental and emotional characteristics — which is his or her constitution. I identify three basic types of energy or functional principles that are present in everybody and everything. They are *vata*, *pitta* and *kapha*.

Ayurveda

This is Ayurveda. Energy is required to create movement so that fluids and nutrients reach the cells, enabling the body to function. *Vata* is the energy of movement, *pitta* the energy of digestion or metabolism and *kapha* the energy of lubrication and structure. *Vata*, *pitta* and *kapha* are permutations and combinations of the five elements present in the cosmos.

I am an optical instrument which was invented by Sir David Brewster, a Scottish scientist, in 1816, and patented by him in 1817. He named me after the Greek words, *kalos* or 'beautiful', *eidos* or 'form', and *scopos* or 'watcher'. So it means the beautiful form watcher. I am a telescope-like visual toy reflecting an endless variety of striking and colourful patterns.

Brewster's instrument was a tube containing loose pieces of coloured glass and other pretty objects, reflected by mirrors or glass lenses, set at angles that created patterns when viewed through the end of the tube. Later, in the early 1870s, an American called Charles Bush improved upon me.

In April 1818, London was surprised by the sudden appearance of an optical instrument for creating and exhibiting beautiful forms. The novelty was so enchanting that opticians could not manufacture them fast enough to meet the universal desire for seeing the delightful and ever-varying combinations, presented by each turn of the magical cylinder.

I consist of a cylindrical body with an eyepiece at one end, mirrors contained in the centre and an object case or wheels at the other end. While viewing through the eyepiece, the viewer may rotate the object case or wheels to change the images reflected and multiplied by the mirrors. The images produced in this comparatively simple device can be startlingly complex, mysterious and fascinating.

Kaleidoscope

This is a kaleidoscope. A small sealed glass container encapsulating coloured liquid, bubbles, micro-beads or other elements to add life and movement to a kaleidoscope's object chamber is called an ampule. **Dichroic glass** showing two or more colours is used by many artists to achieve dazzling effects. Its variation is the **teleidoscope**, which has no moving parts.

Coloured liquid, bubbles and micro beads in the sealed glass tube of kaleidoscope shine bright

In geography, I am an imaginary line drawn around the planet earth, halfway between the poles, where the surface of the roughly spherical planet is parallel to the axis of rotation. In other words, I am a great circle around the earth that is equidistant from the geographic poles and lies in a plane perpendicular to the earth's axis. I divide the surface into the Northern Hemisphere and the Southern Hemisphere.

My latitude is 0° by definition. The length of me as a line is about 40,070 km. I intersect North and South America, Central Africa and Indonesia. On me, the sun is directly overhead at noon on the days of the equinox. Furthermore, every day is close to 12 hours on me. At night, all stars appear to trace out a half circle centred at the southernmost or northernmost point of the horizon. When the sun lies in my plane, day and night everywhere are of equal length — this happens at the **equinoxes**.

Between the March and September equinox, the earth's northern latitudes are inclined towards the sun up to a point known as the Tropic of Cancer, the most northern point where the sun can be directly overhead. The most southern equivalent reached between September and March equinox is named the Tropic of Capricorn.

Seasons in the tropics and at me differ significantly from seasons in the temperate zones. In many tropical regions people identify two seasons — wet and dry. On me, seasons can vary depending on a variety of factors including elevation and proximity to an ocean. In astronomy, the celestial circle is the great circle in which the plane of the terrestrial circle intersects the celestial sphere, thus being equidistant from the celestial poles.

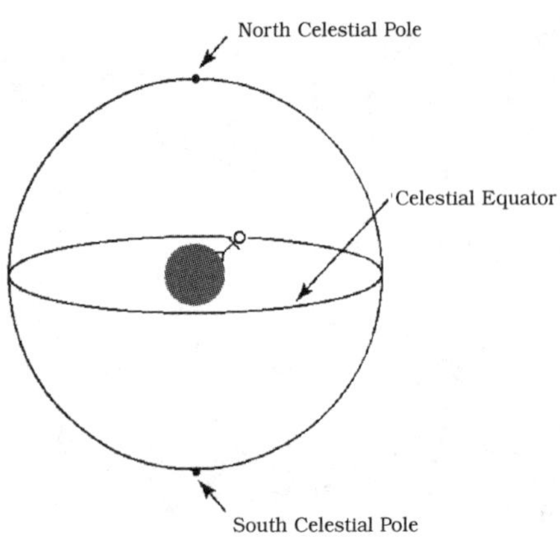

Equator

This imaginary line is the equator. Locations near the equator are good sites for potential spaceports or space elevators, as they are already moving faster than any other point on the earth due to the earth's rotation, and the added velocity reduces the amount of fuel needed to launch a spacecraft. The surface of the earth at the equator is mainly ocean.

I am usually a pair of small removable lenses that can be worn in contact with the eye in such a way that I rest directly on the cornea of the eye. I help correct the wearer's vision without the need of using glasses. Around 1508, Leonardo da Vinci was the first to think of developing me and later on so did René Descartes. In 1887, the German physiologist, Adolf Eugen Fick invented me. He first experimented me on animals and later on made them for the people.

I was initially made from heavy brown glass and measured 18-21mm in diameter. My design was improved by August Muller in 1889 for correcting myopia or nearsightedness. In 1948, an American optician, Kevin Tuohy, made me in plastic for the first time. Around 1970 my soft lens or **hydrophilic** lens as also gas permeable lens form were invented. My earlier forms were uncomfortable for the eyes. I help people suffering from disorders such as myopia, **presbyopia**, hypermetropia and **astigmatism**.

My soft lens version is quite comfortable to wear. I also allow oxygen to penetrate. I need to be disposed daily. I also have ultra thin edges. However, my hard lens form is preferred over my soft lens form since the latter has a high water content. My hard lens form though not so comfortable is durable and provides high clarity vision. A wetting solution is required to use me and I am expensive. My gas permeable lens form lets oxygen to penetrate.

I am made from a polymer which is transparent and flexible. Polymers also have a low density and are hydrophilic in nature. Besides being found in abundance, they are also easy to manufacture and are easily mouldable. Almost any age group can wear me but the elderly find it difficult to use me. Since I have become more affordable and can be easily disposed, my sales have increased. Lots of companies are researching on different types of materials so that I may be used for enhancing my existing properties.

Contact Lens

Contact lenses have fast become very popular. They are manufactured in different colours and designs. They pose a big rival for glasses and have a bright future, particularly for those wishing to change the colour of their cornea.

We are large snow domes which were built as singing, dancing and wrestling competition halls for the community during the long nights of winter by Inuits and Eskimos. Greenland, where the small Inuit community was isolated from everyone, believed themselves to be the only people in the world until the beginning of the 19th century. The Eskimos live in the Canadian Arctic.

Martin Frobisher's 1576-78 expedition to Baffin Island in the Canadian Arctic made the engraving of an Inuit village. The windows of all my snow domes face towards where they will get the most light. When it is winter, the sun never rises for three months; light is by stars, moon and aurorae. Sleds and **kayaks** are hung up, so as to keep them from freezing in the ice. Frobisher's party killed some Inuits and kidnapped one Inuit man, who was exhibited in London like an animal.

My snow domes with braced roof, covered with thick walrus hides, then with dirt, followed by snow serve as winter insulation. People decide who they would live with the following winter during the summer hunt. Winter settlement communities were transient and changing. My snow domes were tightly sealed after the keystone was inserted and a lamp was kindled inside.

The heated air, having no exit, begins to melt the face of the snow blocks, which rapidly congeal again on admission of cold air from the outside. Each snow block is firmly cemented in place and converted to ice on its inner face. The transformation gives it remarkable stability. The doorway is a hole at the feet, which has to be traversed on hands and knees. There is a narrow, roofed passage of snow blocks which has to be passed with head bowed.

Igloos

This is an igloo. Inside, there is a saucer-shaped vessel of stone, filled with burning seal-oil, and with a stone cooking pot suspended above it. A low platform covered with skins occupies half the floor space. There, side by side with their heads facing the door, the inmates sleep in bags or robes of caribou fur.

I am a form of cleaning process that is employed for clothing and textiles by using a solvent other than just water. Chlorinated hydrocarbon solvents are utilised, the most popular being **perchloroethylene**, commonly referred to as 'Perc'. My machine is smiliar to the domestic washing machine. It is much larger in size, so that all the cleaning solvent is captured, filtered, and re-used during my cycle instead of flowing down the drain. Earlier on, petrol was used.

After the Second World War, carbon tetrachloride and trichloroethylene became popular solvents. Perc is considered to be toxic and a long time exposure to it could cause serious liver and kidney damage. I was accidentally discovered in 1855, by Jean Baptiste Jolly, a French dye-works owner. He noticed that his tablecloth became cleaner after his maid accidentally dropped a kerosene lamp on it. I am included during the process of tagging and inspection, pre-treatment, post-spotting and finishing. I am carried out after the process of pretreatment.

In the process of tagging and inspection, small paper tags or labels are written on shirt collars. They are used to help identify clothes owned by different people, so that they do not get mixed up. Also, the clothes are manually checked for missing buttons, tears, etc. during the pre-treatment process. Clothes are checked for stains so as to make their removal easier and better. During my process, the clothes are placed in a machine which cleans them with a solvent. In post-spotting, lingering stains are removed.

Finally in the finishing process, the clothes are ironed, folded and packaged. The use of environmentally safe products has increased in recent years as a result of government regulations and greater consumer awareness of environmental issues. Micell Technologies Inc has developed a cleaning system that uses carbon dioxide (CO_2) technology that is an environmentally safe alternative to the traditional chemical solvents that are used in my process.

Drycleaning

This is the drycleaning process. Dry cleaning began in France about the middle of the 19th century, at first in small plants, where it was done by hand. Now the more advanced machines undertake the process of cleaning.

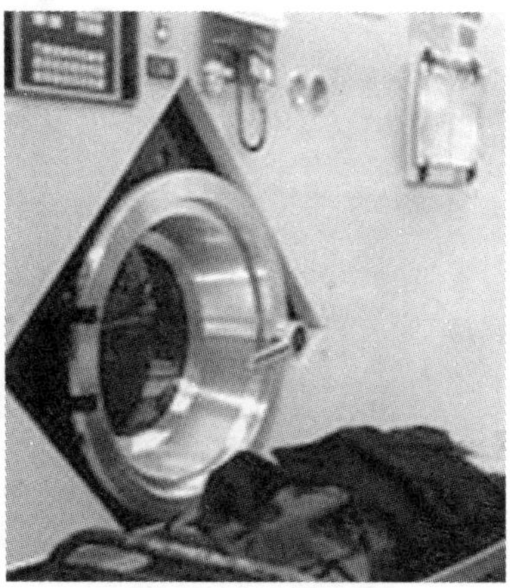

I am an integrated circuit that has all the thinking parts of a computer — a central processing unit, memory, input and output controls, and one small chip. In November 1971, a company called Intel introduced the world's first single chip integrated circuit, the Intel 4004, invented by Intel engineers: Federico Faggin, Ted Hoff, and Stan Mazor.

After the invention of **integrated circuits** revolutionised my design, the only place to go was down — in size, that is. The Intel 4004 chip did this. Programming intelligence into inanimate objects has now become possible. I have made possible the inexpensive hand-held electronic calculator, the digital wristwatch and the electronic games.

In 1968, Bob Noyce and Gordon Moore, two engineers, decided upon the name 'Intel' for their company, a shortened version of 'integrated electronics'. In late 1969, a potential client from Japan called Busicom, asked to have 12 custom chips designed — separate chips for keyboard scanning, display control, printer control and other functions for a Busicom-manufactured calculator.

Intel engineer, Ted Hoff, decided that Intel could build one chip to do the work of 12. Intel and Busicom agreed and founded the new programmable, general-purpose logic chip for use in me. The integrated model of me — the *memory management unit* (MMU) was developed by Childs et al. of Intel and awarded US patent number 4,442,484.

Microprocessor

This is the microprocessor whose invention created a revolution. At 1/8th in. wide by 1/6th in. long and consisting of 2,300 MOS (metal oxide semiconductor) transistors, the baby chip had as much power as the ENIAC, which had filled 3,000 cu ft with 18,000 vacuum tubes. This was the first microprocessor produced by Intel 4004.

I am an alternative system of medicine founded in the early 19th century by a German physician, Dr Samuel Hahnemann. I became very popular in the late 19th century in the United States, when 15 per cent of the doctors in this country practised me as a form of medicine. I first came to widespread public attention through my effectiveness in curing epidemics of cholera in the 19th century.

During the great influenza epidemic after First World War, hospitals practising my form of medicine reported very low death rates, while hospitals employing conventional medicine reported death rates of 20-30 per cent. Since Second World War, the double blind clinical trial has become the 'gold standard' for determining the effectiveness of medical treatment.

The classical form of me rests on three principles: the law of similars, the single medicine and the minimum dose. The law of similars states that a disease is cured by a medicine which creates symptoms similar to those the patient is experiencing when not healthy. Hence, the prescription involves a lengthy interview to determine all the symptoms the patient is experiencing.

The principle of the single remedy states that a single medicine should cover all the symptoms the patient is experiencing: mental, emotional, and physical. The principle of the minimum dose has two parts — first, the physician only prescibes a small number of doses of the medicine and waits to see what effect the medicine has. Second, the medicine is given in an infinitesimal dose.

Homeopathy

This is homeopathy. Homeopaths have discovered that the effect of homeopathic medicines is strengthened upon successive dilutions as long as the medicine is violently shaken between each dilution. Conventional doctors claim it functions only as a placebo. However, controlled studies show the effectiveness of homeopathic medicine in treating certain diseases.

I am an instrument that helps in binding together sheets of paper by driving a thin metal pin through the sheets of paper and then folding over the ends in order to make sure that I do not harm the paper with my sharp ends. I can be easily found in almost every office or any place that processes huge amounts of paper. Before I was invented, people would sew papers together, skewer them with pins, use glue or after punching a hole in them, secure them with a ribbon.

As I eased up the fastening technology, I have been mentioned in the records of history to be used by King Louis XV of France in the 1700s. This particular model had handmade pins with the insignia of the royal court inscribed on it. My first form was in the form of a 'paper fastener'. Sam Slocum patented me on September 30, 1841. This was a very crude form of mine. I would just stick pins on paper to fasten them. Another form of mine could load just a single staple and use it to bind papers, books, carpets.

The Novelty Manufacturing Company patented me on August 6, 1866. George W. McGill developed my small, bendable brass form. In the 1930s, a stationery wholesaler, named Jack Linsky, founded the Swingline. He developed such a form of mine that used pins glued together in a strip. Although it was easy to load, the process was cumbersome. He then soon developed my present form in 1937. In this, one just has to open the top of my machine, and put the pins in. A magazine spring is connected to my top part, mounted on a hinge.

On opening me, I start to pull back the spring and the follow block.The follow block is the piece at the end of the spring that pushes the pins forward. On closing me, I make the follow block to slide back into place against the newly loaded pins. I can be designed to be operated while sitting on a desk or any other flat surface, but many users prefer to pick me up and squeeze my ram head and base together. This way I am slower but more precise.

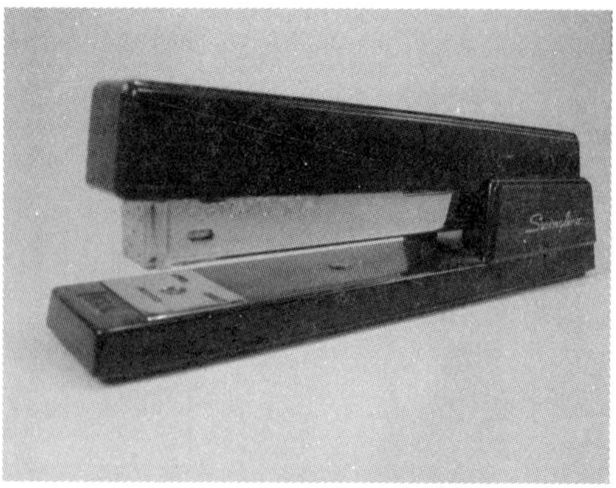

Stapler

This is the stapler that got famous as the Red Swingline Stapler from the movie *Office Space*. In this movie the stapler is the prized possession of an office worker, Milton Waddams, who goes completely insane mainly due to his stapler being frequently borrowed by his boss, Bill Lumbergh.

I am the type of input device that allows the users to operate a PC by simply touching the display screen. Dr Sam Hurst invented the touch sensor, which is my very important component. He worked as an instructor in the University of Kentucky. In 1974, my first true form came into being. In 1977, Elo Touch Systems developed my most popular form, which is still in demand today. I came equipped with a five-wire resistive technology.

Then they patented this design. I can be used for a wide variety of computing applications. I can be easily found with most PC systems like any other input device, such as track balls or touch pads. I have three main components namely, a touch sensor, a controller and a software driver. For my optimum use I need to be used along with a display and a PC or any other output device. A touch sensor has a clear glass panel that responds to touch. It is placed on top of a display screen so that it covers the area that can be viewed by the user on a video screen.

There are many different types of sensor technologies. On touching the screen, the sensor emits an electrical current. The change in voltage is used to decipher the location of the touch on the screen. A controller connects the touch sensor to the PC. I transmit and translate the information from the touch sensor to the PC. I can be found inside the monitor or in a plastic case. Special controllers are also available that can be used with DVD players and similar devices. The software driver allows the sensor and the computer to communicate with each other.

I interpret the information that is sent from the controller to the operating system. Most of my models are mouse-emulation type drivers, i.e. I work the same way as the clicking of the mouse would do on the screen. The software driver also helps me to work alongside the already existing software and this way I do not require the use of any special programme. Thin client terminals, DVD players and a few special computer systems either do not use software drivers or come equipped with their own software drivers.

Touch Screen

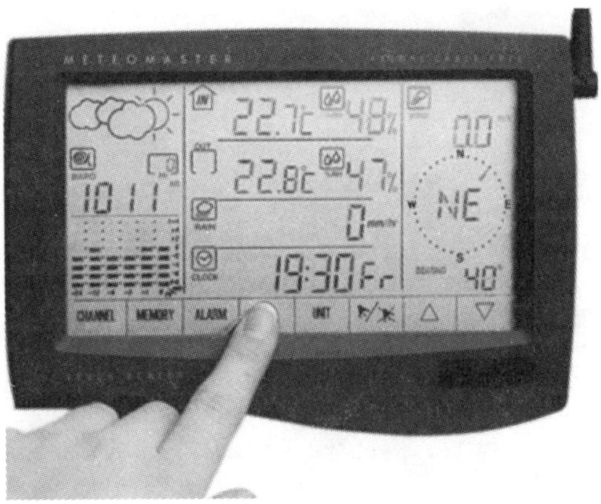

This is the touch screen which is one of the most user-friendly PC interfaces to use, making it a popular choice for a variety of applications. It is used in information kiosks, tourism displays, trade show displays and other electronic displays. It is a favourite amongst those who have little or no computing experience.

I was known to the ancient Peruvian Incas of the Andes who stored their potatoes and other food crops on mountain heights above Machu Picchu. The cold mountain temperatures would freeze the food and slowly vaporise the water inside, under the low air pressure of the high altitudes. I am the process of sublimation or of complete removal of water content from frozen food. Dehydration occurs under vacuum with the plant/animal solidly frozen in the process.

There is no shrinkage. This results in almost perfect preservation. This way the food lasts longer than other preserved food and is very light, thus, making it appropriate for space travel. Shackell worked on my design. He installed an electrically driven **vacuum pump** instead of the displacement of air with ethyl ether to produce the necessary vacuum. I help preserve materials that are unstable in solution.

Also I can be used to separate and recover volatile substances along with purifying materials. My process involves freezing the product since it is very important to do so for low temperature drying. It also involves placing the frozen product in a vacuum. With this, the frozen solvent in the product vaporises without even passing through the liquid stage. This is popularly known as sublimation. After this, the frozen product is heated up in order to accelerate sublimation.

Vaporised solvent is removed by converting it back to solid. My first commercial use was in Second World War as a preserver of blood plasma and penicillin. I involve the use of a special machine that has a large chamber for freezing and a vacuum pump for removing moisture. Since 1960, over 400 different varieties of freeze-dried food have been commercially produced. However, I am not very effective with very high water content food, like lettuce and watermelon. The most popular freeze-dried product is coffee.

Freeze Drying

Freeze-dried coffee was first produced in 1938, and this led to the development of powdered food products. Nestle Company found a solution to Brazil's problem of surplus coffee by inventing the freeze dryer. Nestle also came up with its own freeze-dried coffee product and named it Nescafe, which was first introduced in Switzerland.

I am a vehicle that is paddle-driven. I have two wheels that are attached to my frame, one behind the other. I was first developed in Europe in the 19th century. I had a huge imapct on the cultural and industrial history. Pierre and Ernest Michaux, the French father-and-son team of carriage-makers, invented my modern form in 1861. With my addition to transportation, I multiplied human efficiency by a factor of approximately five.

I have been developed for use in many occupations: in the military, in sports and as a popular form of recreation as well. Leonardo da Vinci is said to have sketched my first form in 1490 but it was not developed. Around 1790, a French craftsman named de Sivrac developed a 'Celerifere' running machine. In this, I had two in-line wheels connected by a beam. The rider would straddle this beam and propel me by pushing his feet on the ground in a scooter-like fashion. In 1817, a German, Baron Karl von Drais, added steering to my form.

Several such models of mine became a popular hobby around France and England by the early 1800s, but my use soon went down as the roads were not pliable. After Ernest Michaux developed my 'Celerifere' form, there soon developed a craze for me. My larger front wheel made me faster but unstable. However, the war of 1812 brought an end to this craze. Soon British engineers further improved my design. They added ball-bearings, pneumatic (Dunlop) tyres, wire-spoked wheels, chain drive, variable gears, and cable controls.

Just over a 20-year span, they developed my present form with the help of James Starley of the Coventry Sewing Machine Company. In 1885, the Starley Rover safety model was born. In this my wheels were of a reasonable size and helped to improve my stability. Almost all my modern models are composed of a two-triangle frame: front triangle and back triangle. My pedals rotate my **crankset** which fits into my bottom bracket. Attached to my crank is my chain-ring that drives my chain, which in turn rotates my rear wheel via **sprockets**.

Bicycle

I am the well-known bicycle, on which the postal services of many countries have long relied for their services. In India, many of Mumbai's *dabbawalas* use bicycles to deliver hot lunches to the city's workers. At the enormous Mercedes-Benz factory in Sindelfingen, Germany, the workers use bicycles that are colour-coded according to their different departments, to move around the factory.

During the Age of Enlightenment in the 16th-18th centuries, philosophers ruminated over the natural rights of all humanity. The right to clean, pure water began to be associated with these innate rights of all humanity. French scientist La Hire developed the concept of every French household having a sand water filter installed. Sand filters became the most popular method of filtering water throughout many European towns.

In 1804, the first citywide municipal water treatment plant was installed in Paisley, Scotland to provide filtered water to every household within the city limits. This Scottish water treatment plant used slow sand filters that were designed by Robert Thom, a Scottish scientist. In 1827, James Simpson, an English scientist, created a similar design to Thom's, and the Simpson water filter models were soon widely used in municipal water treatment plants.

As municipal water treatment facilities sought to increase the quality and healthfulness of public water supplies, they discovered the use of chlorine in their water treatment process. Chlorine was recognised as a valuable chemical in treating cholera-causing water. This application of chlorine resulted in a sharp decline in deaths from diseases such as typhoid, cholera and dysentery. **Chlorination** began in New Jersey and soon spread through the entire United States.

Scientists are now examining the possible by-products and side effects of using chlorine in drinking water since chlorine is considered to be a type of poison. Chlorinated water aggravates and maybe even causes respiratory diseases like asthma. Since it tends to vaporise at a much faster rate than water, chlorinated water presents a significant threat to the respiratory system when used for showering. This has led to many people installing shower filters or whole house water filter systems.

Water Filtration

Development of water filtration became necessary when Anton van Leeuwenhoek discovered tiny living organisms in a drop of water after examining it under the microscope. John Snow, a British scientist, discovered the presence of tiny cholera bacteria, proving that water cannot be declared pure just by judging its appearance; hence, filtration was introduced.

I am an electronic device or a type of transducer that converts acoustic power into electrical voltages. Emile Berliner for Alexander Graham Bell first developed me in the form of a telephone transmitter in 1876. David Edward Hughes invented my carbon model in 1878. My ribbon form was invented in 1942, for radio broadcasting. During the 1970s, my dynamic and condenser forms were developed with a lower level of sensitivity and a clearer sound.

A variety of mechanical techniques can be used for building me. My two most common designs are the **magneto-dynamic** and the variable condenser. In my magneto-dynamic design, the sound waves cause a thin metallic diaphragm and an attached coil of wire to move. A magnet produces a magnetic field, which surrounds the coil; the motion of the coil within this field causes the current to flow. A current is produced by the motion of the diaphragm, and the amount of current is determined by the speed of the coil's motion.

In my condenser design, the diaphragm is mounted in such a way that it almost touches a rigid backplate. This plate may or may not have holes in it. A battery is connected to both pieces of metal, which produce an electrical potential, or charge, between them. The amount of charge is determined by the voltage of the battery, the area of the diaphragm and backplate, and the distance between the two. This distance changes as the diaphragm moves in response to sound. When the distance changes, the current flows in the wire as the battery maintains the charge.

The way I pick up sound from various directions is known as my pickup pattern. Depending on this pattern, I can be any one of these types: omnidirectional, unidirectional, bidirectional and **cardioid**. In my omnidirectional form I pick up sound from all directions. I am usually used for recording ambient and background sound. My unidirectional form is used for recording individual voices in noisy locations, such as interviews. My cardioid form is used on stage.

Microphone

The oldest and simplest microphone uses carbon dust. This technology is still being used in some telephones today. Crystal microphones use the phenomenon of the crystal changing its electrical properties as it changes its shape.

If you were to be lost in the middle of an ocean and had no other celestial bodies like the sun or the Pole Star to guide you in which direction north is, then you could use me to let you know the way. I am the simplest and easiest instrument ever to have been developed to deduce which direction north is. I was discovered in China probably during the Qin dynasty (221-206 BC).

By 9th century I was used as a navigational device for guiding ships of Persian sailors and then the Venetians as I was traded around. I was first designed on a square slab with markings and a loadstone spoon-shaped pointing needle pointing south. Magnetised needles soon replaced the loadstone pointers. Loadstone is a naturally occurring magnetic ore. It was discovered that when an iron or steel needle was touched by a loadstone for enough duration, it aligned itself in a north-south direction.

The Chinese may have used me to reach India for the first time. In the earlier days I would be used to check whether the houses that were being newly built were facing the magnetic north and were in perfect harmony with Nature. Today I am made of a small lightweight needle with one end of the needle marked as 'N' for north. This needle pivots on a frictionless point. Since the earth's core is magnetic, a simple and natural rule of 'opposites attract' makes the north end of the needle point towards south, which in turn makes me point south.

However, the magnetic field on the earth's surface is fairly weak, hence it is very important that I have a lightweight magnet. My drawback is that I may not show the right direction if the platform is unsteady. This has been corrected in my latest form as a **gyroscope** when I am used on board ships and airplanes. I am constructed in such a way that even if the frame moves or rotates, with a motor running inside, I always point towards north. I continue to show the right direction even during turbulent weather conditions.

Compass

The English scholar, Alexander Neckam, described the compass as a 'pointer carried on board (a ship) which enables a course to be followed even when the Pole Star is hidden by clouds'.

I am a form of energy that evolves from the free flow of electrons. Electrons and protons are subatomic particles. They are constituents of the nucleus in every atom. Electrons are negatively charged whereas protons are positively charged. There is a balancing force between these **subatomic** particles. If an outside force disturbs this balancing force, it can bring about changes in the number of electrons. The rise or fall in the number of electrons causes a free flow of current.

I am a secondary form of energy source, that is, I can be produced from converting other sources of energy like coal, natural gas, petroleum and nuclear power. I can also be produced from natural sources of energy, such as water, wind, geothermal power, biogas and solar energy. Earlier people used kerosene lamps for light and to keep their houses warm by burning wood. Now I give power to run devices like computers, light bulbs, radio, television, airconditioners, traffic signals, automobiles, telephones, etc.

In 600 BC, the ancient Greeks noticed that after rubbing amber buttons on fur for a long time, they would attract light objects like hair and even cause sparks. After Dr Benjamin Franklin's famous experiment of flying a kite on one stormy night in Philadelphia, the principles that govern my phenomenon were more easily understood. C. F. Du Fay was the first to discover the two types of me, positive and negative. George Westinghouse invented the transformer to transmit me over long distances to people's homes and businesses.

Michael Faraday, Alessandro Volta, André-Marie Ampère and Georg Simon Ohm studied me closely and formed the basis of my technology. They were honoured by the society by naming the fundamental units of my measurement after them. I am measured in units of power called watt, in honour of James Watt, who invented the steam engine. With my advent, Samuel Morse invented the Morse Code, Thomas Edison invented the phonograph, George Westinghouse invented the locomotive that would run on my energy.

Electricity

In 1600, William Gilbert, an English scientist, came up with the modern Latin word *electricus* from the Greek word *elektron*, meaning amber. Soon the English words 'electric' and 'electricity' were discovered.

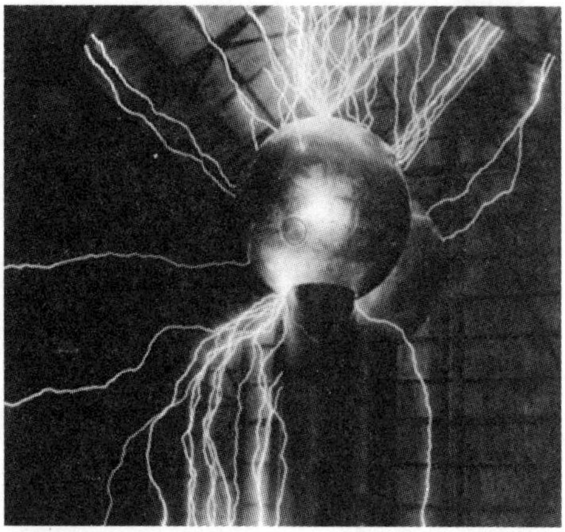

This is the flow of electrons in a circuit. It is slowed due to the resistance in the material.

I am one of the earliest discovered and widely used antibiotic agent, derived from the **Penicillium soil mould**. Antibiotics are natural substances that are released by bacteria and fungi into their environment, as a means of inhibiting other organisms. Due to this property, antibiotics are used to cure infectious diseases caused by bacteria. Alexander Fleming, a Scottish bacteriologist at St. Mary's hospital in London, discovered me in 1928 while researching on lysozyme.

He claimed that his discovery might save lives if it could be produced in quantity. During the Second World War, Fleming, along with two other British scientists, Howard Florey and Ernst Chain, working in the USA, produced the antibiotic on an industrial scale for widespread use. Fleming shared the Nobel Prize for medicine along with them in 1945. Once I became widely available during Second World War, I became a medical miracle, rapidly destroying the biggest wartime killer that would cause deaths and infected wounds.

I am able to kill bacteria by interfering with their ability to synthesize their cell walls. The bacteria can lengthen, but cannot divide. Eventually the weak cell wall disintegrates. However, improper antibiotic use can cause the bacteria to produce antibiotic-resistant pathogens. I am the 'wonder drug' that saves hundreds of lives. Four years after various drug companies began mass-producing me in 1943, microbes began appearing that could resist me. The first bacterium to resist was *Staphylococcus aureusis* that causes pneumonia.

Andrew J. Moyer received the patent for my industrial production. Dorothy Crowfoot Hodgkin was the first to discover my molecular structure. Based on this, other scientists developed other antibiotics. I am not a single compound but a group of closely related compounds, all with the same basic ring-like structure (a beta-lactam) derived from two amino acids (valine and cysteine) via a tripeptide intermediate. My new semi-synthetic forms are Ampicillin, Carbenicillin and Oxacillin. I can cure meningitis, syphilis, tonsillitis, etc.

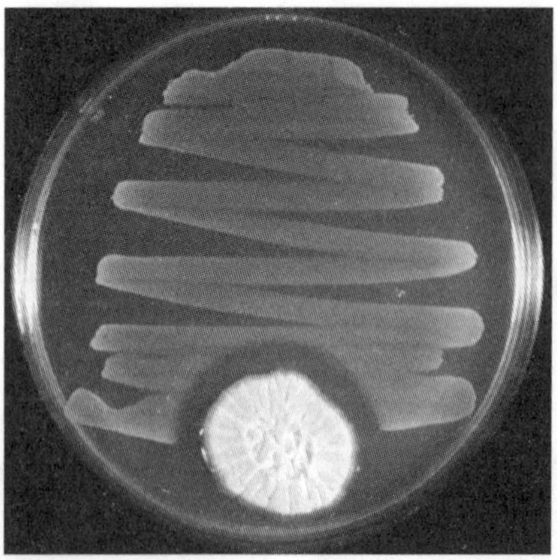

The penicillium mould with the bacteria in the dish.

Penicillin

Penicillin and other antibiotics are used to treat a number of common diseases and prevent the onset of infections. The Chinese were using mouldy soybean curd to treat skin infections 3,000 years ago and some other cultures were using warm earth to treat injuries.

I am an instrument through which one can observe minuscule objects that are too small to be visible to the naked eye. My first model was a simple structure of a tube with a plate for the object at one end and, at the other, a lens that magnified the object 10 times its actual size. Since I let people view fleas or tiny creatures, I was referred to as a 'flea glass'.

Zacharias Jansenn, a Dutch eyeglass maker, once while grinding lenses noticed that some of the lenses made things appear bigger. When these lenses were put together, they magnified things. He then built my first model in 1595 and this could magnify things 20 to 30 times. Another Dutch businessman, Anton van Leeuwenhoek, invented another model of me that would magnify an object up to 200 times. With my help, he was the first one to see the molecular structure of bacteria, yeast plants, the biotic life in a drop of water and circulation of blood corpuscles.

Leeuwenhoek also invented new methods for grinding and polishing lenses that would be used in me. Robert Hooke, an English gentleman, made further improvements on Leeuwenhoek's model. This consisted of a single glass lens of short focal length for the object, and another single glass lens for viewing. He observed a slice of cork and noticed 'pores' and 'cells' in it. Soon, major improvements were made. Several European countries started building better models of me. The best was by an American, Charles A. Spencer.

Now, I magnify objects up to 1,250 diameters under ordinary light and up to 5,000 under a special blue light. My modern versions have multiple lens components in both objective and eyepiece assemblies. I became very popular among the scientists. Joseph Jackson Lister found a way of reducing the '**chromatic** effect' or the halos appearing due to differences in refractive light. He claimed that several weak lenses when used together at certain distances gave good **magnification** without blurring the image.

Microscope

We can view objects as small as the diameter of an atom with the help of the electron microscope. The most powerful microscope to have ever been built is the scanning tunnelling microscope built by Nobel laureates, Gerd Binnig and Heinrich Rohrer.

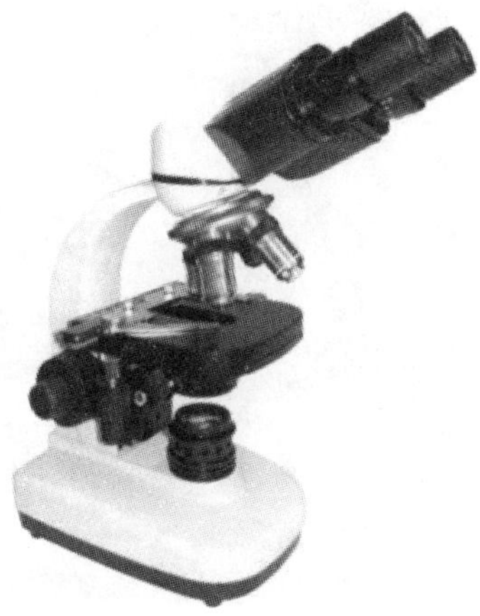

I am a device with which multiple copies of a document can be made by using movable characters or letters. The Chinese, the Japanese and the Europeans were already using me with handset type cast moulds. The Chinese and the Japanese were using wooden blocks to produce Buddhist charms. The Europeans were printing playing cards and even religious illustrations. I brought an end to the arduous task of making multiple copies of manuscripts by hand.

I saved time and effort as documents could be copied in a matter of weeks that would ordinarily take years. Johannes Gutenberg, a German goldsmith and businessman, was the first to invent me with the help of Andreas Dritzehn. I would consist of replaceable wooden or metal letters. I was first used to print the Bible, now known as the Gutenberg's Bible. The invention of the movable-type of me facilitated an easier exchange of ideas throughout Europe and led to a fall in the price of printed material.

I helped popularise and spread the ideas of the Renaissance. I brought about changes in the literary world due to mass production. Before I was invented, publications mainly consisted of illustrations with short captions. So the literate class had to largely depend on handwritten documents. The ink was rolled over the raised surfaces of hand-set letters held within a wooden form before it was pressed against a sheet of paper. Within 30 years of my invention in 1453, my use spread all over the world

The Times of London introduced the first steam model of me, in 1814. Ottmar Mergentahler invented my linotype model, in 1884. The **monotype** model was first used in 1897. It made typesetting easier. Gutenberg also developed methods for mass production of paper. Paper was brought from China to Italy in the 12th century. Prior to the use of paper, books were made of vellum (calf or lamb skin) because of its durability. He also developed oil-based inks. The letters would be put together in a type tray that was then used to print a page of text.

Printing Press

The invention of the printing press helped in the advent of the scientific revolution, in the acceleration of Protestant reformation, raising the literacy level, revolutionising education and eventually, in the formulation of copyright laws.

I am a device that converts the potential energy that exists as pressure in steam, and converts it to mechanical force. I brought about the Industrial Revolution. I was not a big hit in automobiles since I took 30 seconds to develop pressure. My first model was in the form of a toy and was invented by Hero, a Greek philosopher and mathematician, before 300 BC. He observed that the expansion of water vapour could be harnessed to provide enough energy so as to move an object.

I was a sphere with two spouts that rotated on a hollow axle connected to a boiler. After about 1,000 years, the Marquis of Worcester in 1640, Denis Pain in 1687 and Thomas Savery in 1698, each tried building me but their versions were slow and cumbersome. Savery was the first person to find a practical utility for me. His model helped pump water out of coal mines. James E. Watt, a Scottish engineer, made a lot of improvements and developed my first practical form in 1769. Watt and his business partner started my large-scale manufacture.

I can be of various types but mostly of reciprocal piston or turbine variety. Since the oxygen for combustion is not metered, I am able to burn fuel cleanly and efficiently, with relatively little pollution. I had one major drawback since the condenser would cause losses by being somewhat hotter than the outside environment, thus, causing inefficiency. James Watt solved this problem by introducing steam jacketing, oil lubrication and a separate **condensing chamber** to maintain high temperature.

With my help, nuclear energy can be harnessed for useful work, as a nuclear reactor does not directly generate either mechanical work or electrical energy. I provide power to factory equipments, such as spinning machines. After the Industrial Revolution, I was used widely in locomotives and steamships. I brought a lot of changes in the life of the people since I could provide power to run other machines. In a steam locomotive when the valve of my cylinder is opened, I release a steam exhaust. As the steam escapes with pressure, I make a '*choo*!' sound.

Steam Engine

The steam locomotive, the steamship, factories, all depended on the steam engine to get them working. Today the steam engine has largely been replaced with electric and diesel engines but still remain a source of fascination due to their heritage charm.

I am the product of combustion. I am the brilliant light, glow and heat produced when the self-sustaining **exothermic process** of oxidation takes place, when combustible gases are released from a fuel. I can be induced by subjecting a fuel to an incredible amount of heat or source of energy, such as a matchstick and can be sustained until the entire combustible fuel is exhausted. I have been credited for bringing about civilisation.

However, before humans knew the ways of creating or controlling me, I posed as a terrible threat to humankind for a long period. I could be moved around and my magnitude could be changed but humans had no clue on how to revive me. Eventually, around 5,000 BC, once mankind realised my potential powers, they set about finding a way to control me. They were successful in finding the means of starting me. This occurred almost everywhere around the world.

They began to use me to make their surroundings more warm and bearable and to produce light in darkness. This made it possible for people to migrate to colder areas. The first few methods of starting me included rubbing two pieces of wood vigorously together. Then it was discovered that I could make the raw food more edible and last longer after cooking it. I was then used as a weapon and then finally for smelting metal and ceramics. In lots of cultures, I play a significant role in their religious rites and rituals.

In some parts of the world they still worship me. Such as in Hinduism, I am considered as one of the five sacred elements that all living creatures comprise of. I am a constant and also represent God in the Zoroastrian rituals. However, I can cause serious damage to all living as well as non-living beings and objects. If proper standards are not maintained while building structures or proper arrangements are not made for extinguishing me, I could annihilate everything, as could happen in cooking accidents, electrical faults and leakage in gas.

Fire

Fire has been feared, venerated, tended, controlled, extinguished, recreated and most often, used over the centuries by almost every civilisation that ever existed on this planet earth.

I am considered as one of the most important products used in offices all over the world, after the paper clip. My efficiency and versatility is the reason for my ubiquity. The thought of developing me occurred to Arthur L. Fry in the early 1970s while he was searching for an appropriate bookmark for his church hymnal. His colleague, Dr Spencer Silver, who was a senior chemist, invented a type of me that was strong enough but would leave no residue when removed.

Thus I could be reused. When applied I would acquire the form of tiny spheres. I could not be dissolved or melted easily but would stick well. My inventor, since he had always been a problem solver, thought of applying some of me on the edge of a piece of paper and then using it as a bookmark. From then on he would use me to communicate with his other colleagues by leaving me sticking to a file. He would also use me to organise his work. Soon the idea of using me caught on with the rest of his colleagues.

Thereafter the 3M Corporation started mass-producing me for sale. Today I can be found on almost every file, computer, desk, bulletin board, school, lab, library, office and home. Initially, the 3M Corporation almost gave up on the idea of selling me. Geoff Nicholson, an employee at 3M, managed to convince Joe Ramey on my utility. Judging by everyone's response, they finally agreed on taking up the project of producing me for commercial use. I made a strong impact on the market right in the first year itself.

I was declared as the Company's outstanding new product. From then on, there have been many innovative products that were developed using me. I can be found in the form of a note **dispenser** and tiny flags. It took five years to develop me with the perfect specifications and to design the right type of machines to produce me. In 1980, I was introduced to the world. Both, Arthur Fry and Spencer Silver won numerous awards in the international engineering community.

Post-it Notes

A new software has been developed that behaves like the all-important post-it notes on computer desktops. Post-it notes are one of the most reliable and reusable office supply products for leaving behind messages or to convey instructions.

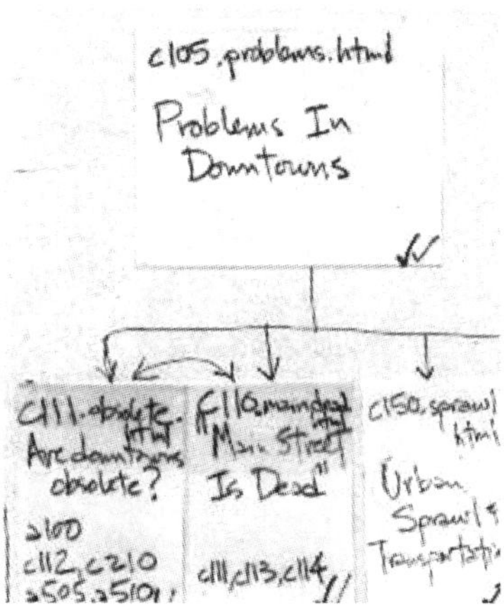

I refer to the process of making identical copies of an original and in the biological sense, I refer to the process of copying genes and chromosomes to propagate other identical material. There are other branches of me that can be used to recreate identical animals. The naturally occurring process of reproducing twins involves the splitting of the embryo after fertilisation. Each embryo would carry DNA from both the parents, thus resulting in identical twins.

I, on the other hand, can produce an animal that would carry DNA of only one parent. With the process of somatic cell nuclear transfer, scientists can transfer the genes of the nucleus of an adult sheep's udder cell to an egg, whose nucleus does not carry any genetic material. Somatic cells are those cells that are not egg or sperm cells. As a result, a group of Scottish scientists were able to develop a sheep, Dolly, in 1997. A few South Korean scientists have recreated human embryos with my help.

The 'host' egg cell develops into an organism genetically identical to the nucleus 'donor', since its nucleus now would contain an exact copy of the genetic material from the 'donor' cell. Even if some mitochondrial DNA is not transferred properly by me, it is generally overlooked as is does not have any drastic effects. I have been debated, analysed, and scrutinised the world over. In some countries, I have been banned while in some I am legal. With my help, humans have been able to make duplicates of sheep, mice and cows.

I can be used as a medical aid for helping people cope with severe medical problems such as in recreating human organs and parts. I could also be used to fix disease-causing mutated genes, like in cancer. I have also been approved for helping in curing diseases like Parkinson's and Alzheimer's. For this, by using me, they can grow neurons or nerve cells. I facilitate them to grow stem cells. These stem cells are then further used to recreate organs like the heart, liver and skin. I can be used for helping couples who want to have a child.

Cloning

The word ***clone*** is of Greek origin; it means 'twig' in Greek. Clone is a group of genetically identical cells descended from a single common ancestor, such as a bacterial colony whose members arose from a single original cell as a result of **binary fission**.

I was first invented in 1813 by Peter Durand for the British Army. The cans that I would be packed in were made of solid iron and weighed too much. During the Napoleonic wars, Napoleon's army often suffered from casualties arising due to malnutrition rather than during battle. Once this was observed, new methods for preserving the nutrients in food were developed. The French government offered an award of 12,000 francs to anyone who could solve this problem.

Nicolas Appert, a French baker and brewer, came up with a solution, one which he had been experimenting for over 14 years. He claimed that if fresh food were to be packed in airtight containers and a certain amount of heat was applied, the food would stay healthy. He unwittingly managed to sterilise the food since he submerged the packed containers in boiling water, thus inhibiting any bacterial growth. Peter Durand made further improvements in this method. Bryan Dorkin and John Hall perfected the design for the tin containers I would be packed in.

As providing the armies with healthy provisions became a priority, I was in greater demand. Thomas Kensett immigrated to the United States and established the first US canning facility for oysters, meat, fruits and vegetables in New York in 1812. After 50 years, Louis Pasteur explained my effectiveness as he had observed the growth of micro-organisms as the cause of food spoilage. Heat sufficient enough to destroy harmful **micro-organisms** is applied to foods packed in sealed containers.

The time for processing largely depends on the level of acidity, density and ability of the food to transfer heat. For example, tomatoes require less time than green beans, while corn and pumpkin require far more time. Care is taken to ensure that I retain my flavour and nutrition. Usually I am able to retain my purity for two years. I am safe to consume unless I get punctured and am not kept airtight any more. I am packed at the peak of my freshness. The canneries that pack me are usually situated near the sites of harvest.

Canned Food

Canned food has become commonplace now. It was a novelty when it was being used to feed undernourished soldiers in Napoleon's army. It is a process of sealing cooked food for future use. Highly acidic food is packed in boiling water.

The idea of inventing me occurred to Frank X. McNamara, head of the Hamilton Credit Corporation while lunching with his friends. They were discussing the problem he was facing with customers who had borrowed money from him but were unable to pay it back and this particular customer landed in trouble, when he lent a number of his charge cards to his poor friends needing some items. They in return were unable to pay back the loan and the interest charged.

When it was time for McNamara to pay for the lunch, to his horror he realised that he had left his wallet behind. So he asked his wife to bring him some money to pay off the bill. He was then struck with the novel idea of combining the two issues and solving two problems: the problem of money lending and the problem of getting caught in a situation of carrying no money, once and for all. He thought of inventing me so that I could be used anywhere and at anytime when the need arose for money.

After discussing his brilliant idea with his friends Alfred Bloomingdale and Ralph Sneider, they went ahead and pooled in some money and started a new company, called Diner's Club. Diner's Club would act as the middlemen. They replaced the structure of individual companies giving credit to only a few customers by Diner's Club giving credit to individual customers for many companies. After that they began to charge the customers and pay back the companies.

I used to be made of a paper stock with the accepting locations printed on the back. Now, I am made of plastic. I am issued to a customer only after the initial approval of the issuing bank. After a purchase is made, the customer gives his/her consent by signing a receipt. This purchase can be made within the credit limit. I carry a strip of magnetised material wherein I carry important information that can be electronically verified. I am also used on the net or over the phone by quoting the number that is embossed on me.

Credit Card

This is the convenient and easily accessible credit card that can be used almost anywhere in the world. It also helps the customer to keep track of all the transactions made on his card.

I was invented over a century ago. I can support both axial and radial loads and withstand some amount of misalignment of the inner and outer races. In some of my models, **spherical bearings** are used as rolling elements and in others, just a single ball suffices. By using a well-calibrated version of me, humans were able to grind in a day what would normally take them a week to achieve. I brought about the invention of the bicycle. I enabled the wheel to be used for bringing mobility.

I acted as an aid for augmenting the efficiency of humankind all over the world, since I helped save lots of time and effort. A man can travel three of four times faster than the pedestrian but use five times less energy in the process. In my radial model, I use inner and outer races that are shaped so as to let the load pass radially through me. I also support modest axial loads. In my angular contact model, I use offset races. An angular load passes in a straight line through me, whereas a radial load passes in an oblique path.

An axial load is transmitted directly through me while a radial load is poorly supported. In a deep-groove model, the race dimensions are close to the dimensions of the balls that run in me. I have higher load ratings than the shallow-groove bearings. My most popular industrial form is the deep-groove Conrad style. In this, the inner and outer races are placed radially offset. This way, the races touch at one point and have a large gap on the opposite side. Balls are placed in the large gap. A cage is inserted to hold the balls in their places.

I have been named after my inventor, Robert Conrad. Most of my designs are single row designs and some are double row designs. The double row designs need better alignment as compared to the single row designs. Mostly bicycles use the shallow-groove Conrad style. My roller model is used in conveyor belt rollers. My ball-thrust model is used for bar stools. My tapered roller model is used in car hubs. My giant roller model technology is used for making buildings earthquake proof. I am also used in columns supporting the weight of airports.

Ball Bearing

Probably the use of the ball bearing can be dated back to the time when the Egyptians were building the pyramids. They would put round logs under heavy stones so that they could roll them over to the building site.

The American Seventh Day Adventists were the first to develop the concept of producing a commercial wholesome cereal food, back in the late 19th century. I am a member of the grass plant family. There are different types of cereals, like wheat, rice, oats, barley and corn. Will Keith Kellogg, the founder of the W.K. Kellogg Foundation, was trying to find a way to improve the vegetarian diet of patients recuperating in hospitals.

Will Keith Kellogg's brother, Dr John Harvey Kellogg, was the superintendent of a sanatorium in Battle Creek, Michigan. While experimenting with a pot of boiling wheat, both the brothers **serendipitously** discovered me. He observed that when rolled and dried, each grain of wheat would turn into large thin flakes. These flakes were more than just edible. They were tasty and highly nutritious. I am made from a combination of corn, sugar and vitamins.

The dough is then rolled, toasted and formed into flakes. I can be served with milk. I am very popular as a breakfast cereal, since I am easy to make and tasty to eat. In 1906, Will Keith set up his own company Kellogg's and started mass-producing me. I was their first product to be marketed. In 1909, he added special offers like giving out comic booklets with every purchase of their cereal boxes. This continued for 23 years. There have been other popular characters that children all over love to collect.

Along with enjoying their favourite cereals every morning, the children would look forward to Tony the Tiger, Trix the Rabbit and many more such characters. Will Keith Kellogg soon became a cereal industry giant. The thought of making me from corn developed mainly due to the fact that corn was a very important part of the daily American diet, especially in the southern regions of the country. Hominy was a popular dish among the native Americans. It is made by mixing corn meal mush along with corn pone and grits.

Cornflakes

In his quest for finding a suitable digestible bread substitute for his brother's patients, Will Keith Kellogg discovered cornflakes. Since then, cornflakes has been a favourite breakfast cereal of many all over the world.

My original form was the abacus that was developed in China in the 9th century. Blaise Pascal, a French mathematician, developed the first version of me in 1642. I would perform mechanical addition and subtraction with the help of gears. William Seward Burroughs built the first commercial model in 1886. Otto Steiger built the first adding model of me that would do simple mathematical calculations like multiplication, in 1894.

I am a device used for numerical calculations. Texas Instruments incorporated (TI) in 1966, invented my hand-held pocket version. In 1974, my miniature electronic version was patented by Texas Instruments incorporated. I was personal-sized and would run on battery. My main electronic circuit would be in a single integrated **semiconductor** circuit array. I was later on developed into a 'one chip' model. In 1958, Texas Instruments invented my integrated circuit.

I was later patented in 1964. This then led to a dramatic change in the design of almost all electronic devices. I would contain all the necessary electronics that can perform addition, subtraction, multiplication and division. I would sometimes come equipped with a keyboard consisting of 18 keys and a visual display in the form of a semi-conductor thermal printer that would print out calculations upto 12 decimal digits. I have been developed into more complex models. In older times, people would use comptometers and Napier's bones to calculate.

They were tedious and time consuming. Now, I am widely used in my electronic form. I can be battery powered or solar powered. I can be found in various shapes and sizes. I can be a cheap miniature model or a sturdier model with built-in printers. However, there are very few companies that have developed my latest forms for professional and financial use. I perform basic mathematical functions and even complex trigonometric calculations. In my latest models, I can be programmed to display graphics.

Calculator

The first calculator to be invented was Pascal's calculator, way back in 1645. It was greatly used for calculating taxes in France until 1799. IBM invented the first all-transistor calculator. The first pocket calculator with scientific functions was developed by Hewlett Packard.

I am a weapon that obtains energy from nuclear fusion or **nuclear fission**. Usually my simpler forms derive energy from nuclear fusion and my more complex and developed forms derive energy from nuclear fission. In nuclear fission a mass of fissile material reaches a critical mass in which a chain reaction takes place. Critical mass would mean the amount needed for a self-sustaining nuclear chain reaction. As it grows, it releases energy.

In the case of nuclear fusion, the X-ray thermal radiation from a nuclear fission explosion heats up and compresses a capsule of tritium or lithium resulting in nuclear fusion, thus, releasing a great amount of energy. This particular form of mine is called hydrogen bomb. When the nucleus of uranium-235 absorbs a neutron, it undergoes nuclear fission, splits into two 'fission' products and releases energy. In my more advanced forms, I am detonated by the blast of a neutron bomb.

The energy that I release is measured in terms of kilotons and megatons of TNT. My 'Strategic' variety is used to set off larger weapons meant to destroy larger targets, such as cities. My 'Tactical' variety is used to destroy specific military, communications and infrastructural targets. This particular form is lighter and more compact. My mobile ballistic model can be delivered over a range of hundreds of kilometres. I can also use suborbital or partial orbital trajectories for the intercontinental range. As a cruise missile, I have a shorter range.

I can be carried by a jet aircraft or a rocket-propelled missile that would fly at a low altitude, using an automated guidance system. I can be launched from mobile launchers on the ground, from naval ships and aircraft. The United States developed my first fission form during Second World War. India conducted its first atomic explosion in 1974. India also tested my fission and fusion devices in 1998. My uranium-based 'Little Boy' was let loose on the Japanese city of Hiroshima, on August 6, 1945, killing thousands of people.

Nuclear explosion producing a large cloud of smoke and debris.

Nuclear Weapon

Nuclear weapons cause mass destruction and are powered by atomic rather than chemical process. Nuclear weapons produce large explosions and hazardous radioactive by-products. They create radioactive contamination that can continue to cause cancer and birth defects for years.

I am a bottle that prevents the transfer of heat from the inside to the outside and conversely to a minimum. This way, I am able to maintain the temperature. I keep warm drinks warm and refrigerated drinks cold. In other words, I provide very good thermal insulation. Sir James Dewar, a Scottish chemist and physicist, at the University of Cambridge, developed me in 1892. He built me with the intention of studying low temperature gas phenomenon.

Dewar wanted to know as to how gases turn into liquid. For this reason, he would use me to maintain the temperature of the liquids. He would mostly use me to transport liquid hydrogen. Earlier on, I would be made of glass and now I am made of metal. Thus, I am more durable and damage resistant. I comprise of a thin outer container and a thin inner container, which are separated by a vacuum. This **vacuum** makes sure that the heat transfer due to convection or conduction is reduced. The two containers are sealed together at the neck.

My interiors as well as exterior are usually silvered. This would further reduce radiant heat transfer. Very little amount of heat could be transferred through the neck and the stopper. An insulating material like cork is used for the stopper. The German company Thermos GmbH adapted Dewar's invention and went about mass-producing me for commercial and home use, in 1904. I am commonly used to store liquid nitrogen in laboratories. A low temperature has to be maintained to keep nitrogen from boiling up.

Hence, a special pressure relief valve has been designed and installed to prevent pressure from building up. Since I am able to maintain the inside temperature and pressure, I am also used for keeping beverages, like coffee and tea, hot. Since my glass models are expensive to make and easily perishable, other materials such as plastic and insulated metal are also used. I was then named after my inventor as the Dewar flask.

Vacuum Bottle

A local from Munich, Germany came up with the idea of naming his adaptation of the Dewar flask as 'Thermos'. He was inspired by the Greek word *therme* meaning 'hot'. Now, Thermos GmbH uses it as a trade name for its flasks.

Numerous breakthroughs coupled together set forth my development. Photography and sound recording are my quintessential elements. Without them, I would not be around. I was discovered when the realisation dawned on people that a series of closely spaced sequential pictures, if viewed in rapid succession, would give an illusion of movement. Leonardo da Vinci studied this phenomenon.

This resulted in the development of hand-held devices in which a person could view images on a spinning wheel or a spinning disk. Before my advent, people entertained themselves by watching shadow plays, using lanterns and animated puppets.This particular form of entertainment was very popular in India, Indonesia, the Middle East and then it spread to Europe. Joseph Plateau in Belgium and Michael Faraday in England, both studied the importance of the psychology behind the persistence of vision.

Plateau developed the spinning slits of the **phenakistoscope**. Sequence photography was successfully conducted by Eadweard Muybridge. They would use images that were printed on opaque surfaces for direct viewing. I evolved when William Friese-Greene in England and Thomas Alva Edison in the United States went about printing multiple images on a transparent surface that could be projected. George Eastman had developed the nitrocellulose film rolls that were being used for still photography.

It was patented in 1891. The Lumiere brothers, Auguste and Louis developed the cinematograph, which was an improved version of the kinetograph. This then further led to my full-scale projection on a theatre wall at the Grand Café in Paris on December 28, 1895. Edison developed an even better projector, the Vitascope. It first projected me at a theatre in the United States at Bial's Music Hall in New York City, on April 23, 1896. Later on, William Dickson built the biograph, which projected sharper images.

Pictures taken within seconds of each other and then projected at a fast speed to produce animation

Motion Picture

Motion pictures are a form of art, entertainment and business. Sound films were initially referred to as talkies. The use of colour in films was the final major development in the field of motion pictures. The Indian film industry is the biggest film industry since it produces the maximum number of films in a year.

I am used in first-aid. Earle Dickson, an employee at Johnson & Johnson invented my ancestor in 1921. He was inspired to do this by his wife, Josephine Dickson, who was always cutting her fingers in the kitchen while preparing food. Earle Dickson had noticed that gauze and adhesive tape would soon fall off active fingers. He decided to create something that would stay in place and protect small wounds better.

Dickson took a piece of gauze, attached it to the centre of a piece of tape, and then covered the product with crinoline to keep it sterile. His boss, James Johnson, saw Earle Dickson's invention and decided to manufacture it for the public. Earle Dickson was rewarded with vice-presidentship of Johnson & Johnson.

Now-a-days, I am available in the market in many shapes and one can use me conveniently. I am better known in many parts of the world as an adhesive or a sticking plaster. I am a trademark used for an adhesive bandage with a gauze pad in the centre employed to protect minor wounds.

These readymade types of me can be used on cuts directly. It was a boon for the public in a world full of cuts, scrapes, blisters and bruises. Today, the doctors are against me being used on wounds because the latest belief doing the rounds is that natural healing by keeping the wound exposed is the best treatment.

Band-aid

This is band-aid or brand adhesive bandage. The first adhesive bandages were produced and sold under the world-famous BAND-AID® trademark.

I am a common fire-starting device. I consist of three parts, namely a head that is made of phosphorous and is easily combustible; a tinder substance that is usually a piece of wood to pick up or burn the flame; and a handle that is most often the same as tinder. People all over the world had discovered that by rubbing two sticks together or with flint, due to friction, would spark up a fire.

In 1680, Robert Boyle, an Englishman, observed that phosphorus and sulphur would immediately burst into flame if rubbed together. After conducting experiments, he went on to realise that they would catch fire not because of friction but due to their inherent chemical nature. This led to my discovery. By the early 19th century, various chemical fire-starting devices were being developed and used in Europe. Some of them involve the phosphorus/sulphur combination and others would involve gaseous hydrogen, which was risky.

John Walker, an English physicist, invented my first form in 1827. He used sulphuretted peroxide on enormous yard-long sticks. Then my phosphorous form was first commercially used in Germany, in 1832. I was extremely hazardous for human life. Alonzo D. Phillips of Springfield, Massachusetts patented this form of mine in 1836. He named me 'locofocos'. Carl Lundstrom of Sweden developed my first red phosphorus form in 1855. This form was relatively safer to use.

To save himself from the embarrassment of carrying a bulky box of wooden strikers, he thought of producing books of my paper form that could be easy to carry. His concept received a boost when the Mendelsohn Opera Company used books of my paper version with their names imprinted on it in order to advertise their New York opening in a special way. The Diamond Match Company patented my first non-poisonous version using the harmless chemical sesquisulphide form of phosphorous.

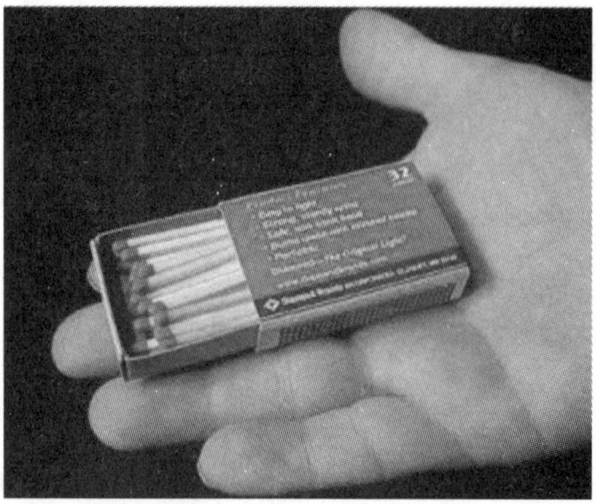

Matches

Before the advent of the match, small pinewood sticks using sulphur were being used in China in 577. Gustaf Erik Pasch in Sweden invented the safety match in 1844. The matchbox was developed in the United States in 1890.

I am a type of lethal explosive chemical. For a long time, gunpowder used to be the only workable explosive until I was discovered. Ascanio Sobrero, an Italian chemist in 1846, invented the explosive chemical, nitroglycerine. Doctors also use nitroglycerine as a heart medication. Its natural liquid form was highly unstable and volatile. Although it was highly unstable, it would take very long to detonate in cold weather.

In 1866, Alfred Nobel, a Swedish engineer, after losing his father in an explosion in his family's nitroglycerine factory in Heleneborg, Sweden, went on to study me and discovered my malleable paste form that could be achieved by mixing nitroglycerine with silica. He improved my efficiency in cold weather by mixing nitroglycerine with **trinitrotulene** or TNT. J. Wilbrand in Sweden invented TNT. I would be shaped in a cylindrical form that could then be inserted into the drilling holes used for mining. In 1867, he patented me.

He set up many factories all over the world that would produce me. I played a major role in the industrial development of the world. I am used for blasting canal beds, mines, quarries, roads, railroads, levelling land for housing, foundations for constructing buildings. I am also used for demolition in warfare. I am usually stuffed into cartridges made either of plastic or wax paper. A detonating cap is placed inside one end of the cartridge. I am then placed inside the material that needs to be blasted. A fuse or an electric current is used to set off the cap.

I have four different varieties and they are namely: straight, ammonia, straight gelatine and ammonia gelatine. The straight form is my oldest form. My ammonia form is stronger, safer and cheaper and more commonly used. In this form, I produce cooler gases and fewer toxic fumes. For this reason, I am used in mines where extreme heat can cause the gas or dust in the air to ignite. My ammonia gelatine form is water-proof and is therefore used in underwater, hard-rock blasting. I have not been used commercially for quite some time.

Dynamite

Alfred Nobel invented the dynamite. He used all the money he received for his invention and founded the prestigious Nobel Prize to be awarded to leading physicists, chemists, scientists, all over the world. The word 'dynamite' comes from the Greek word *dynamis*, meaning 'power'.

I am a type of material that can fasten objects together. George de Mestral, a Swiss engineer, invented me in 1948. After returning from a hike with his dog, he noticed that burrs or tiny plant seed sacs, had attached themselves to the dog's fur so that they could be transported to fertile lands. On examining one of these burrs that got attached to his trousers under the microscope, he noticed that they were viciously stuck to the tiny loops in his pants.

This was when he was struck with the idea of inventing me. He wanted to build something that would act as a two-sided fastener. On one side there were stiff hooks and on the other, there would be soft loops. With the help of a weaver in France, he went about developing me. By fluke, he noticed that nylon when sewn under an infrared light would form into tough hooks. He then patented me in 1955. He formed the now multi-million-dollars-worth industry and started my mass production. He was able to sell 60 million yards of me.

I consist of two nylon strips. One strip has thousands of small hooks and the other contains small loops. Once these two strips are joined, they form a strong bond. When these strips are separated, they make a distinct ripping sound. Although strong, I can be easily separated. I am light weight, durable and washable. I can be found in a variety of colours. There is no problem of jamming, as happens in the case of the zipper. My efficiency depends on how well the hooks are embedded in the loops and the force with which they are pulled apart.

When I am used in bonding rigid surfaces like automobile body panels and frame, the bond is extra effective, since the force that pulls the pieces apart is spread evenly across all hooks. There are three methods to increase my strength. One way is to ensure that the force applied is parallel to the plane. The second way is by increasing the area of the bond; and the last method is to use a pulley system like in the case of shoe closures. I have a few drawbacks. I tend to collect hair, dust and fur in my hooks after a few months of regular use.

Velcro

Full-body Velcro suits have been made that can hold a person to a Velcro-covered wall. De Mestral got inspired by the French words *velours*, meaning 'velvet', and *crochet*, meaning 'hook'. Velcro is used in designing space equipments that are used by astronauts to prevent them from floating away.

It is difficult to get through the day without using me even once. I am involved in your daily routine in almost every respect. Whether you are punching in at work, filling up your car at the petrol pump, using your cellular phone or paying for your meal, almost always I will be involved some way or the other. The French inventor, Roland Moreno, is usually credited for inventing me in 1974. Today I contain an integrated circuit.

I can store data up to 4 KB. Thus, I provide better security than the magnetic strip cards. Since I am dependent on external hardware, I am best suited for a few operations: I am known as the chip card; I store data as well as process it; I can feature 8-bit processor, 16 KB ROM and 512 bytes RAM that make me as effective as the old desktop computer. Due to my processor and additional memory, I am able to perform a great many memory and security related tasks involving maintenance of information regarding secure digital identity.

I use modern semiconductor technology to increase the amount of data that can be stored in me. Also, my microprocessor, complete with busses and **interface**, further adds to my memory storage function. This way I can carry out basic encryption functions with great ease. All my major manufacturers prefer using the secure platform-independent Java as the language in my applications. I am used as an insurance card. For this purpose, I contain a detailed medical history of my user, spanning several years.

I am used as a prepaid phone card. I can also identify my user's cellular phone. Since I can uniquely identify each individual user, I am best suited for financial applications, such as negotiating a huge number of monetary transactions. I enable my users to log into their bank accounts through an ATM machine to pay electronically, using a point-of-sale terminal. I can be used as a navigational card that authenticates my user and allows him or her to travel on trains and metros, free of the hassles of purchasing a ticket every time.

Smart/Swipe Cards

This is the smart card now in common use in cities and towns. In Europe, they are now trying to develop a new type of technology that would involve absentee voting via the internet. In Germany, a secure electronic processing of tax returns is being developed.

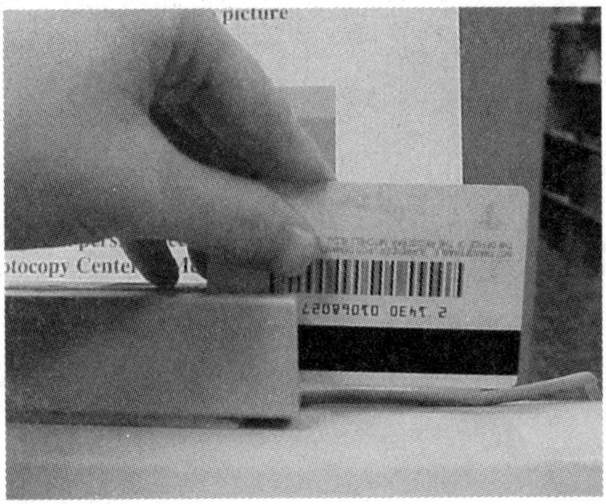

I am a very practical conveyor type of transport device that transports people. I can be described as a moving flight of stairs that moves up or down with the help of a **conveyor belt** at a 25 degree angle. I was initially built for amusement by Jesse Reno from Massachusetts in 1859. I was driven by steam. I acted as a novelty ride at Coney Island. Reno patented me, the 'moving stairs', on March 15, 1892.

Charles Seeberger further improved my design in 1897. Seeberger, with the help of the Otis Elevator Company, started mass-producing my first commercial model at the Otis factory in Yonkers, New York. I was made of wood. I also won the first prize at the Paris 1900 Exposition Universelle in France. The Otis Elevator Company bought Seeberger's patent rights over me, in 1910. They also bought Jesse Reno's patent in 1911. Soon enough, they went about enjoying a monopoly over my production.

They made further improvements in my design. David Lindquist and other Otis engineers developed my cleated, level steps that are in great use today. I comprise of floor plates that level with the finished floor. These are either hinged or can be easily removed to allow for easy access to the machine spaces under me. I have a comb plate, which is a piece attached between the stationary landing and my moving step. It would slightly slant down in order to fit properly between my **cleats** and steps.

I have a mechanical truss that bridges the space between my lower and upper landings. It can be described as a hollow box that is made up of two side sections. These sections are joined together with transverse braces across the bottom and just below the top. The truss rests on concrete or steel supports. A track system is constructed into the truss so as to guide the step chain, which then pulls the steps through an endless loop. This way, the steps appear to originate from under the comb plate to form a staircase that moves.

Escalator

Charles Seeberger thought of the name 'escalator' from the Latin word *scala* meaning 'steps'. Otis lost their product trademark of 'escalator' after the United States Patent Office made it a rule that the word escalator had become a generic term for describing moving stairways.

The idea of inventing me can be traced back to the 1st century in Rome, where Vitruvius Pollio studied the use of a counterweight and pulley system to transport people up and down a building. Louis XV had installed one of my oldest versions at Versailles. I was called the 'fly chair'. I would be powered by human, animal or even water-wheel power. Around the middle of the 19th century, I was steam operated and used for conveying material in factories, etc.

American inventor Elisha Graves Otis patented my first practical and safe model in 1851. In this, I was equipped with a safety device to keep from falling in case one of the supporting cables were to snap apart. Otis then went ahead and formed his company to start manufacturing me for commercial use. He patented my steam model in 1861. Sir William Armstrong installed the **hydraulic** crane in me. In this model, a heavy piston moves in a cylinder and is operated by water pressure produced by pumps supporting me.

My car is raised and lowered by six or eight wire ropes that are attached to the top of the car. They are motor-driven wires and they travel around a pair of sheaves, which are also attached from the other end to a counterweight. This counterweight is of great use since it acts as an accelerating force when my car is ascending and on other hand, it acts as a retarding effort when the car is descending, thus, using less motor power. Usually a bunch of metal weights, equal to the weight of the car, act as a counterweight.

A set of chains that loop from the bottom of the counterweight to the underside of my car helps in balancing me by offsetting the weight of the suspension ropes. Guide rails running on the length of the shaft keep my car and my counter-weight from swaying as they travel. Rollers are attached to my car and counterweight to provide smooth travel. In order to have a precise control over my speed, I use a direct current motor. My newer models use a static drive control. When my car reaches its destination, a switch near the landing signals my destination.

Elevator

In the United States, this is known as the elevator, in Britain it is known as the lift and in France it is known as the ascenseur. The Otis safety elevator was first demonstrated at the Crystal Palace Exposition in New York City in 1854.

I am one of the most basic tools to ever have been devised that is used in almost all complex mechanisms. The idea of using me was known way back in the prehistoric times. The Greek mathematician, Archimedes, described my use in great detail around 260 BC. I can be described as a rigid rod that pivots on an appropriate fulcrum. I am able to multiply the mechanical force that is applied to another object.

Force applied at one end of me can be balanced by an appropriate amount of force that is applied at another point. This point is usually opposite the fulcrum. The closer the fulcrum is placed to the object being raised, the lesser amount of force is needed to lift it. The basic principle that governs me can be understood by Newton's laws of motion. Depending on the position of my fulcrum and the differences in the input and output forces, I can be of three types.

My Type 1 model includes a seesaw, a crowbar, a pair of pliers and a pair of scissors. My Type 2 model includes the wheelbarrow, nutcracker, and the handle of a pair of nail-cutters. The human arm, a pair of tongs, a catapult and tools like the hoe or the scythe are all examples of my Type 3 model. This goes to show that the **fulcrum** can be placed at one end instead of in the middle. In my Type 1 model, the fulcrum is placed in between the effort and the load.

However, when the load is larger than the effort, as in the case of the pliers, the object is moved through a smaller distance. In my Type 2 model, the load is placed in between the fulcrum and the effort, whereas, in my Type 3 model, the effort is placed in between the fulcrum and the load.

The round wheel is the fulcrum on which the hook on one end and object to be weighed on the other end of the chain are the forces.

Lever

The catapult or ballistae, an ancient weapon of war that was used for hurling objects, works with the help of a lever. While explaining the mathematical principle of levers, Archimedes said, 'Give me a place to stand, and I can move the Earth.'

My history can be traced back to ancient times. *Horology*, or the science of telling the time of day, began about 3500 BC with the advent of the **gnomon** and the sundial. They worked efficiently during the day but were quite useless during the night. The ancient Egyptians used clepsydras to tell time. It would run by flowing water. It was a type of hourglass that would use water dripping between two containers that were marked to indicate the passage of time.

Their accuracy was hampered by changes in temperature, weight and water pressure. Yi Xing, a Chinese monk, invented the precursor to my first mechanical model in AD 725. Gerbert d'Aurillac, a French Benedictine monk, is credited for inventing my first mechanical form. I involved a system of gears run by counterbalanced weights. All my older forms were large and had fixed mechanisms. Filipo Brunelleschi, an Italian architect, developed my portable, spring-driven form in 1410.

Christiaan Huygens, a Dutch inventor and astronomer, observed the almost constant oscillation of the pendulum and used it to further improve my precise time-telling capacity. So he went about inventing my first pendulum form in 1657. He determined the mathematical formula that related the length of my pendulum to time. He also developed the balance wheel and spring assembly that can be found in my more recent models. William Clement built me with the 'anchor' or 'recoil' escapement in 1671 that improved my efficiency.

Alexander Bain, a Scotsman, developed my first electrical form in 1840. My quartz crystal form improved my timekeeping capacity much more than that of my pendulum and balance-wheel **escapements**. When a quartz crystal is placed in a suitable electronic circuit, the interaction between mechanical stress and the electric field vibrates the crystal, thus, generating a constant frequency electric signal that is finally used to operate me. Frenchman Louis Cartier developed me in a form that could be worn on the wrist.

Clock

John Harrison created the first, highly accurate marine chronometer. The clock can be found in every home, office, public place, on cellular phones and even on the VCR. It is an instrument other than the watch for measuring or indicating time; it can be a mechanical or electronic device.

I am a visual instrument with frames that bear lenses and aid in correcting the human vision. I used to be made from glass but now I am mostly made from plastic to avoid breakage. I was first invented by Alessandro della Spina, a Dominican friar and Salvino degli Armati, a physicist, in Florence, Italy, in 1280. My first use was to correct far-sightedness also, known as hypermetropia or presbyopia, with the help of convex lenses. This is a common ailment of old age.

I used to be worn only by the very well educated or rich noblemen in Italy. I was made from a variety of materials including wood, lead, copper, bone, leather, and even horn. The Chinese are sometimes credited for developing me about 2,000 years ago, but apparently my only purpose was to protect their eyes from an evil force, or so they believed. I first used quartz lenses until the time optical lenses were discovered. My use spread from Italy to Germany, Spain and France.

In 1604, Johannes Kepler explained in great detail in his treatise on optics and astronomy, the use of convex and concave lenses in correcting vision. In the 17th century, Spanish makers of me tried experimenting by tying silk ribbons to my frame so that I could be looped around the ears. The Chinese attached little ceramic or metal weights to the strings instead of making loops. In 1730, a London optician named Edward Scarlett perfected the use of rigid sidepieces so that I could rest atop the ears. This perfection augmented my rapid use.

Far-sighted or aging colonial Americans imported me from Europe. I was a valuable and treasured appliance for the affluent and literate colonists. In 1784, Benjamin Franklin, an American scientist, invented my bifocal version since he suffered from both presbyopia as well as myopia or short-sightedness, and was tired of switching glasses every time. In this, I have a combination of both concave and convex lenses for both types of vision correction.The top lens is for distant viewing and the lower lens is for reading.

Spectacles

Corrective glasses help in alleviating problems like myopia, presbyopia or hypermetropia. Saftey glasses are made from shatter-resistant plastic lenses so as to protect the eyes from flying debris. Sunglasses provide protection from very bright and ultraviolet light. There are special glasses that create an illusion of three dimension and are used to view 3-D movies.

I am a ship or a special watercraft that travels under the surface of the water. I am employed by most of the major navies of the world. My basic concept was thought of by Leonardo da Vinci. My closest ancestor would be the Ukrainian Cossack riverboat called *Chaika* that was used underwater for **reconnaissance** and infiltration missions. I was actually invented in 1620 by Cornelius Jacobszoon Drebbel, a Dutch inventor and engineer employed by the British navy.

I am also employed to work in depths that is difficult to reach for human divers. Until the advent of nuclear marine propulsion, I mostly used batteries for running underwater and petrol or diesel engines on the surface and to recharge the batteries. My size and range can vary anything from a small two-men vessel to examine the sea-floor, to a huge vessel that can carry many people and remain submerged for many months. I am used to carrying nuclear missiles that can be deployed to destroy hundreds of cities.

I am widely utilised for carrying out military operations since I am very difficult to detect as a I lie very deep below the surface. Hence, I am more difficult to destroy. A great deal of effort has been made to design me in such a way so that I travel through water silently and go undetected. This way, I am able to reach my victim and then strike at a close range. My cigar-shaped or 'tear-drop hull' design has ben inspired by the shape of a whale. It helps in reducing the hydrodynamic drag and makes me move faster.

I can generate oxygen for the crew by electrolysis of water. I have a raised tower on the top that houses a periscope, radio, radar, electronic warfare and other systems. In my older versions, the control room would be normally located inside this tower. I was widely used by the Germans in the North Atlantic during First World War and the US Navy used me to successfully block out the Japanese during Second World War. During the Cold War, the United States of America and the Soviet Union built large fleets of me.

Submarine

The first submarine and first military submarine was the Turtle. It was a hand-powered spherical contraption designed by David Bushnell for the American Revolutionary War. Military submarines are of three types: ballistic missile submarine, guided missile submarine and attack submarine. North Korea is reported to have the largest fleet of submarines.

I am a tool with a sharp edge that is used for removing hair. During the Stone Age, the Neanderthal man first started pulling hair, painting, and tattooing his body. He would also file down his teeth for some reason, too. Ancient cave paintings go on to prove that the early man discovered other ways to remove hair from his face; in the beginning, he would simply pluck them out by using two seashells as tweezers.

To this day, tweezers have remained throughout history as the most popular grooming tool to ever have been invented, used by both men and women to painfully remove body and facial hair. Before my advent, flint blades were used for shaving. The flint would become dull very soon and was therefore disposed off very quickly. The **Neanderthal** man would carve interesting patterns into his skin with the help of these flints and apply natural dyes on these designs. This resulted in tattoos. I was invented some time around 3000 BC.

My first version was made from copper. I was available in India and Egypt. In 1200 BC, I was elaborately designed in Scandinavia. I would be carried in a leather carry-case. Mythological characters and scenes were etched or embossed on my bronze blades and my handles were carved in horse-head shapes. Alexander the Great made shaving a popular habit since he was obsessed with shaving. The Greeks then started considering shaving as an important part of their daily hygiene regimen. Around 500 BC I became very popular with Romans.

Publicus Ticinus Maenas, a wealthy Greek businessman, brought professional barbers from Sicily to Rome, inducing a whole new craze for shaving. They would use thin-bladed iron knives, which were sharpened with water and a whetstone. I was being used in India around 400 BC. I was introduced in Europe during the Middle Ages. The Aztec Indians would make me from volcanic glass obsidian. During the 18th century, England started producing my straight steel versions. King Camp Gillette invented my disposable blade form.

Razor

During the First World War, Gillette worked out a deal with the US armed forces, to provide safety razors and blades to all the recruits on way to Europe as a regular part of their standard issue gear. Alexandre Horowitz, a mechanical and electrical engineer at the Philips Company, in the Netherlands, invented the first double-headed electric razor.

I am a unique puzzle that has only one correct solution and millions of wrong ones. The idea is to solve me in the least number of moves. I am one of the most popular puzzles in history. I have 26 individual little cubes or cubies. Each layer of nine cubies can twist and the layers can overlap. Any three squares in a row, except diagonally, can join a new layer. I was invented so that each of my blocks would move independently without falling apart.

My inventor hand-carved and assembled the little cubies together. He marked each side of the big cube with adhesive paper of a different colour and started twisting. This is how I was invented in the spring of 1974, in Budapest, Hungary, when my 29-year old inventor realised that it was not so easy to realign the colours to match on all six sides. He was not sure if he could ever return his invention to its original position. He theorised that by randomly twisting the cube, he would never be able to fix it. He figured out the answer by aligning the eight corner cubies.

He realised certain sequences of moves for rearranging a few cubies at a time. After a month or so, he was able to solve me. He patented my form in January 1975. A small toy-making cooperative in Budapest started producing me by the end of 1977. My antecedents are the *tangram*, which was developed in ancient China; it consisted of five triangles, a square and a parallelogram — the simple elements that yield a multitude of interesting figures. The *pentomino*, invented by Solomon W. Golomb had 12 different elements and each was made of five squares.

It displayed the possible **configurations** of the five combined squares. Piet Hein's Soma cube was a three dimensional version of *pentominos*. It resembled me both in shape and in the large number of ways its seven elements could be assembled into a 3 x 3 x 3 cube. My 54 outer surfaces of the individual elements were given their colours. Different patterns, numbers and symbols and diverse colour combinations were tried, but none worked as well as the six distinct colours. Euro Rubik invented me.

Rubik's Cube

The Rubik's cube made its international debut at toy fairs in London, Paris, Nuremberg and New York in January/ February, 1980. Minh Thai, a 16-year-old Vietnamese student from Los Angeles won the world championship for solving the Rubik's cube in 22.95 seconds, in Budapest, in June 1982. No one has been able to solve the puzzle in less than 52 moves.

I am a revolutionary technology that enables man to get engrossed in a computer-generated world to get the feeling of experiencing something real. Special software and equipments, like data gloves and head-mounted displays help to create an environment where almost anything is possible. I use computer graphics, sounds, and images to reproduce electronic versions of real-life situations. Jaron Lanier was one of the pioneers of my technology.

I use computerised clothing to synthesise reality. The user can interact and manipulate with the environment that I create with the help of standard input devices, like a keyboard or specially designed cybergloves. My head-mounted display is equipped with a set of wide-angle optics that cover almost the entire horizontal field of view. As and when the user moves his/her head, the image shifts to create an illusion of movement. My data glove has a key interface device that uses position-tracking sensors and fibre optic strands on each finger.

This allows the user to manipulate objects existing within the virtual environment, just as he would do with a real object. My non-immersive form uses a normal monitor and the user can play with a **joystick** inside the virtual ambient. Another way to experience me is by using the method of 'the cave'. It is a room with graphics projected from behind the walls that then surround the person in the room. It gives a feeling of isolation from the rest of the world. The images take the user to a whole new environment.

The user can pretend that he/she is on the moon, in the sky, or out in the middle of an ocean. My programmes help a prospective buyer to take a tour of a house he/she is interested in buying by letting the buyer enter the house without actually being there. For this reason, I am a favourite among the architects since I enable them to view their architectural design before being built. I can be anything the designer wishes me to be. I am of great help to scientists, doctors, pilots etc.

In a computer-generated picture, the viewer feels the aeroplane moving towards him.

Virtual Reality

The term virtual reality was coined by Jaron Lanier in 1989. It is popularly known by its abbreviation 'VR'. Virtual reality has been a big hit in movies and was highly popularised by '*The Matrix*' movie. Flight **simulators** have revolutionised pilot training. Some day scientists may explore celestial bodies and check out lakes beneath the Antarctic ice-pack using VR applications.

I am a colourless, odourless and shapeless fossil fuel. I am combustible and release huge amounts of energy when ignited. However, I am a clean burning fuel. I do not emit any harmful by-products into the atmosphere. I am a mixture of hydrocarbon gases. I am formed mainly of methane, about 70-90 per cent. I also include ethane, propane, butane and pentane. I can be delivered to homes in my purest form.

Ethane, propane and the other hydrocarbons commonly associated with natural gas have slightly different chemical formulae. I am usually referred to as 'dry' if I consist of mainly methane. If other hydrocarbons are present, then I am known as 'wet'. I am found in reservoirs underneath the earth surface. I am commonly associated with oil deposits. Production companies locate me and drill wells in the earth with the help of sophisticated technology. Once I am brought from underground, impurities like water, gases, etc. are removed.

In fact, some hydrocarbons, such as propane and butane, are removed and sold separately. Other impurities like hydrogen sulphide are also removed which, when refined, produce sulphur. After refining, the clean natural gas is transmitted through a network of pipelines, running for thousands of miles. From these pipelines, natural gas is delivered to its point of use. I have been formed from organic matter such as the remains of plants or animals that have been compressed under the earth at very high pressure over time.

I am a major source for electricity generation with the help of gas and steam turbines. My compressed form is used as an alternative for automobile fuel. Countries like Argentina, Brazil, Pakistan, Italy and India have the largest number of automobiles that use me. I am used in houses for cooking and heating too. I am commonly used in rural areas. I also aid in the production of fertilisers like ammonia. A strong smelling chemical like **ethanethiol** is added to me so that leaks can be detected by the smell in order to avoid any explosions.

Natural Gas

The Chinese are reported to have used natural gas in certain regions as early as the 4th century BC. In America natural gas was known to the natives who observed it emitting out from the ground along the western side of the Appalacian Highlands. Natural gas has been utilised in Assam and Gujarat since the 60s.

Gas being past through pipes from the drilling site.

I am a system of conserving and protecting water resources. Water is the most precious natural resource on our planet today. The Indian government has adopted me through its local bodies to conserve rain-water and protect existing water resources like lakes, irrigation tanks, temple ponds, drinking water ponds, etc. Creating public awareness on this issue has been difficult, but then necessity is the mother of invention.

To encourage my use, a refundable deposit is collected from all applicants to be refunded after verification of my structure. I have been made mandatory in certain government buildings. Local body officials and engineers have been specially trained to use me. Temple tanks and other water-harvesting sites are given special preference. Gravel and mud from all irrigation tanks are removed for implementing me. So far permission has been given for over 100 irrigation tanks to save them from encroachment.

The water resources potential in the northeastern region of India is largest due to its heavy rainfall. It has an abundance of groundwater resources. Maximum scope for development of groundwater exists in Assam, Tripura and Arunachal Pradesh. The available surface water resources have hardly been tapped because of the rugged nature of the terrain. In Nagaland there is a system that combines water conservation with forestry, agriculture and animal care.

Aizawl has more than 10,000 harvesting tanks in individual houses, which have been constructed by the residents at their own expense or with state government assistance. In a pollution-free state like Mizoram, where major industries are yet to come, rain-water is free from undesirable chemicals and is of potable quality. Buildings are constructed with sloping roofs that use corrugated **galvanised** iron sheets as these are conducive for implementing me. Meghalaya taps stream and spring water by using bamboo pipes to irrigate plantations.

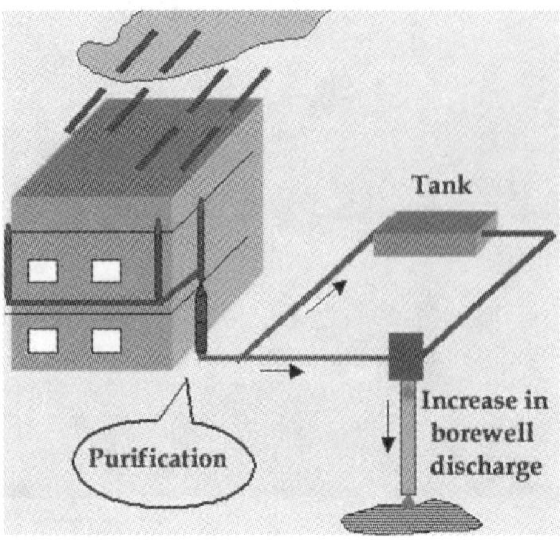

Rain-water Harvesting

Rain-water harvesting is the most important harvesting practice in human life today. To meet the acute shortage of water, especially in the scorching heat of the summer, rain-water harvesting is indispensable for survival.

I am a form of hydropower. Like solar and wind power, I am both natural and renewable. My power stations use fast-flowing water to turn turbines, like windmills use the wind to turn their turbines. The kinetic energy of the flowing water is converted into me with the help of a water turbine that drives a generator. I account for 20 per cent of the world's energy use. My large-scale production was made possible with the invention of electric power transmission in 1820.

I am usually generated from water flowing downhill. For this, I am generated at dams or other places where water descends from a height, or flows with a large tidal swing. My magnitude depends not only on the volume but on the difference in height between the source of water and the water outflow. It is advantageous to build dams on heights so as to produce me in large quantities.The water falls through a pipe called a **penstock**, which then applies pressure against the turbine blades to drive the generator to produce me.

In another system, called run-of-river, instead of falling water, the force of the river current applies pressure on the turbine blades to generate me. Among all renewable sources of energy, I am most widely used. The mechanical energy of flowing water was earlier used to turn a paddle wheel to grind grain. My first industrial use took place in 1880 when 16 brush-arc lamps were powered using a water turbine at the Wolverine Chair Factory in Grand Rapids, Michigan. Since my power source is water, my power plants must be located on a water source.

Therefore, the technology to transmit me over long distances had to be developed to facilitate my widespread use. Hydroelectric plant design became fairly well standardised after First World War with most development in the 1920s and 1930s being related to thermal plants and transmission and distribution. I am one of the most environment-friendly form of generation. I am renewable and an emission-free source of energy.

Hydroelectricity

Norway produces virtually all of its electricity from hydro, while Iceland produces 83 per cent and Austria produces over 70 per cent of its requirements. Itaipu in Brazil, Guri in Venezuela, Sayano-Sushenk in Russia, Churchill Falls in Canada are the world's largest hydroelectric power stations. India's hydro capacity is 82,237 GWh.

Water of the flowing river turns the turbine to convert kinetic energy of water into electricity.

I am obtained from the kinetic energy of wind with the help of wind turbines. Around 1-3 per cent of sun's energy is converted into wind energy. Most of this wind energy can be found at high altitudes where continuous wind speeds of over 160 km/h are common. The sun heats up the earth's surface unevenly. This then powers a global atmospheric convection system that reaches from the earth's surface to the stratosphere, that acts as a ceiling.

Along with the sun, different seasons, change of day and night, land and water temperature, humidity and friction of wind, together affect the flow of wind. The power in wind is extracted by having it act on moving wings, connected to a rotor, which converts some of the power into torque on the rotor. The amount of power transferred depends on the wind speed (cubed), the swept area (linear), and the density of air (linear). The mass flow of air that travels through the swept area of a wind turbine varies with the wind speed and air density.

Albert Betz, a German scientist, determined in 1919 that a wind turbine can extract at most 59 per cent of energy that would otherwise flow through the turbine's cross section. Actual efficiencies can range from 10-20 per cent for propeller-type turbines, and can be as high as 35 per cent for three-dimensional vertical-axis turbines like Darrieus or Gorlov. Since kinetic energy increases with the cube of wind speed, most of the average power available to a windmill comes in short bursts.

A well-sited wind generator has an annual load factor of as much as 35 per cent. Local winds are precisely monitored for a year or more with anemometers. Thousands of wind turbines are operating in various parts of the world, with a total capacity of over 47,317 MW, of which Europe accounts for 72 per cent. India ranks fifth amongst the wind-energy-producing countries of the world, after Germany, Spain, USA and Denmark.

Wind Electricity

In India, by AD 2012, the projected wind power installation is likely to be around 5,000 MW. Wind energy costs are continuously decreasing due to technology development. Germany is the leading producer of wind power with about 35 per cent of the world's capacity to generate electricity.

I am an optical disc that is used for storing digital data. My original purpose was to store audio data. I consist of several stereo tracks that store data using 16-bit PCM coding at a sampling rate of 44.1 kHz. My audio version has a diameter of 120 mm, which is designed to hold 74 minutes of audio. I was later developed to be used as a data storage device, known as CD-ROM. In 1979, Philips and Sony decided to join forces, and they set up a joint task force of engineers.

Their mission was to design my new digital form. Prominent members of the task force were Kees Immink and Toshi Doi. After a year of experiments and discussion, the task force produced the 'Red Book', my standard. I began to be sold in the market by 1983, thus bringing about the digital audio revolution. My user-recordable form for data storage, CD-R, was introduced in the early 1990s, and it became the de facto standard for exchange and archiving of computer data and music.

My later extensions have been extremely successful. I am constructed from a 1.2 mm-thick disc of **polycarbonate** plastic coated with a much thinner aluminium layer, which is protected by a film of lacquer. Originally gold was used in place of aluminium. The lacquer can be printed with a label. The common printing methods are **silk-screening** and offset printing. I am available in two sizes, though my most common form is 120 mm in diameter, with a 74-minute audio capacity and a 650 MB data.

I am also available as 80 mm discs — a format used for my audio versions. In this form I can hold 21 minutes of music, or 180 MB of data. The information on my standard form is encoded as a spiral track of pits moulded into the top of the polycarbonate layer. The areas between the pits are known as 'lands'. Each pit is approximately 0.5 microns wide, a minimum of 0.83 microns long and 125 nanometres high. As the drive motor spins me inside the player, the tracking system focuses the laser on these pits to read the data stored.

Compact Disc

James T. Russell invented the digital compact disc in the late 1960s. He wanted to build a system that would record and replay sounds without physical contact between its parts. He got the idea from digital recording in punch card or magnetic tape form. He saw that if he could represent the binary 0 and 1 in dark and light, a device could read the information stored without ever wearing out.

I am an object that is specially created to play with. I can be found in a variety of sizes and styles, with moveable arms and legs, in character costumes, or with motto/announcements printed on small-sized clothes. My most popular forms are the Teddy Bear and the sock monkey. I can be made after being stuffed with straw, beans, cotton and other such material.

Around the 19th century, I was usually made out of old, homemade cloth remnants and stuffed with straw. Now, with the help of modern technology I am produced in synthetic materials. For this reason, I am also known as a plush toy. The Steiff Company that was specially founded in Germany in 1880, started creating me for commercial use, so much so that in some parts of Germany, my type were popularly called Steiftiere.

Teddy bear was created after being inspired by an incident when Theodore Roosevelt encountered a baby black bear while on a political trip to Mississippi in 1902. This so enchanted the owners of a candy store in New York that they created a replica of the bear, and placed it in their display window. Soon, they were inundated with orders for the Teddy bear, which they had named for the President.

The baby boom of the 1950s stimulated a massive demand for Teddy bears to entertain babies, young children and adults as well. I am very popular due to certain aspects of human psychology. Humans have the natural tendency to nurture and protect young animals as well as children. In the urban environment in modern industrial societies, humans have almost no contact with animals except with their pets. Thus, human curiosity has led to creation of my animal forms, such as elephants and parrots.

Stuffed Toys

Beanie Babies are one of the most popular stuffed toys. They are filled with plastic pellets or beans. They are mostly shaped in the form of animals such as cats, dogs, pigs, giraffes, etc. and are mostly preferred by adults, rather than by children.

Glossary

P. 1
Insulation batts: The high-performance fibre-glass batts, which can significantly improve the energy efficiency of walls and cathedral ceilings and achieve higher R-values without necessarily adding to the cost of building a home.

P. 2
Thermoscope: An instrument for conveying changes of temperature without indicating the degree of heat by which it is affected; especially an instrument contrived by Count Rumford which, as modified by Professor Leslie, was afterwards called the differential thermometer.

P. 3
Psychometric formula: Pre-cut pieces of fibre-glass insulation batts may have a facing of paper or aluminum foil.
Centrifugal refrigeration: When designing the chiller and chilled-water systems, understanding the factors that affect system-operating costs will help in maximising overall system efficiency. The total brake horsepower required by a centrifugal refrigeration machine is directly related to the polytropic head and refrigerant weight flow and inversely related to compressor efficiency.

P. 4
Barometric: The barometric formula, sometimes called the exponential atmosphere, is a formula used to model how the pressure (or density) of the air changes with altitude. It is based on the simplifying (not very realistic) assumption that the temperature does not depend on altitude. However, this formula agrees reasonably well with the actual pressure and density variations above the earth's surface up to a height of about 140 km.
Topography: Topography, a term in geography, has come to refer to the 'lay of the land', or the physio-geographic characteristics of land in terms of elevation, slope and orientation.

P. 5
Crusades: A series of military expeditions by European Christians against Muslim powers between 1095 and 1291, aimed at gaining control of Jerusalem. In all, eight crusades were launched and it was the abortive eighth crusade (1270) which led to the fall of Acre in 1291 and the loss of outposts on the mainland, ending the era of the Crusades.
Siege of Paris: The siege of Paris lasting from September 19, 1870 to January 28, 1871 brought about French defeat in the Franco-Prussian war and led to the establishment of the German Empire. As early as August 1870, a Prussian army marched towards Paris, but was recalled to deal with French forces accompanied by Napoleon III himself. After crushing these forces at the Battle of Sedan, the Prussian army led by Wilhelm I and Helmuth von Moltke was free to move towards Paris virtually unopposed.
Tourniquet: A compression device used to cut off the flow of blood to a part of the body, most often an arm or leg. It may be a special surgical instrument, a rubber tube, a strip

of cloth, or any flexible material that can be tightened to exert pressure. Compression should not be maintained for more than 20 minutes at a time because of the danger of congestion and gangrene. In cases of a bleeding emergency, a tourniquet is used to stop the flow of blood if other means, e.g., the application of a pressure bandage to the wound, are not effective. In arterial haemorrhage (bright red blood spurting out in jets) the tourniquet is applied above the wound, i.e. between the wound and the heart. In haemorrhage from a vein (an even flow of dark red blood) the tourniquet is applied below the wound, i.e. away from the heart.

P. 6
Toroidal: A coil of insulated wire in a doughnut shape (usually with a core of iron or similar metal) is an example of a toroidal object. These are used as inductors in circuits such as low frequency transmitters and receivers because they possess higher inductance and carry greater current than similarly constructed solenoids. They are also used as transformers in main power supplies. Toroidal coils reduce resistance, due to the larger diameter and smaller number of windings. The magnetic flux in a toroid is confined to the core, preventing its energy from being absorbed by nearby objects.
Electrostatic principle: The laws of physics teach that 'like' electrical charges repel one another and 'unlike' electrical charges attract one another. Using this principle, let's construct a conceptual electrostatic speaker. First, stretch a thin plastic membrane on a rigid frame. Then, coat it with a low-mass electrically-conductive substance. Next, fabricate two stiff, flat electrodes, called the stators. They are insulated to prevent electrical discharge. We give each stator the same area as the membrane and place one on either side of it. The membrane is placed exactly equidistant between the two stators. Finally, the stators must have holes in them to permit sound to pass through. We now have a primitive electrostatic speaker.

P. 8
Snorkel: A tube through which a submarine or diver can draw air while underwater. When in use, the top of the snorkel tube extends above the water surface into the air. The first modern snorkel was devised by Leonardo da Vinci at the request of the Venetian senate. It consisted of a hollow breathing tube that was attached to a diver's helmet of leather. The present-day diver's snorkel is typically a J-shaped tube that is open at the top and has a mouthpiece at the other end. Usually no more than 61 cm long, the snorkel can only be used as a breathing device when a diver is swimming face down near the surface.

P. 9
Hydrolysis: A chemical reaction of a compound with water, usually resulting in the formation of one or more new compounds. The most common hydrolysis occurs when a salt of a weak acid or weak base (or both) is dissolved in water. Water ionises into negative hydroxyl ions (OH-) and positive hydrogen ions (H+), which become hydrated to form positive hydronium ions (H3O+). The salt also breaks up into positive and negative ions.

P. 13
Deflagration: Deflagration is a process of subsonic combustion that usually propagates through thermo-conductivity (hot burning material heats next layer of cold material and ignites it). Deflagration is different from detonation that is supersonic and propagates through shock compression.

P. 14
Electrolyte: An electrical conductor in which current is carried by ions rather than by free electrons (as in a metal). Electrolytes include water solutions of acids, bases, or salts; certain pure liquids; and molten salts. Gases may act as electrolytes under conditions of high temperature or low pressure. All inorganic acids, bases, and salts are electrolytes. Electrolytic substances are classified as strong or weak according to how readily they dissociate into conducting ions. An electrolyte is decomposed when a current passes through it.

P. 18
Vapour compression cycle: Vapour compression refrigeration cycles specifically have two additional advantages. First, they exploit the large thermal energy required to change a liquid to a vapour so that we can remove lots of heat out of our air-conditioned space. Second, the isothermal nature of the vaporisation allows extraction of heat without raising the temperature of the working fluid to the temperature of whatever is being cooled. This is a benefit because the closer the working fluid temperature approaches that of the surroundings, the lower is the rate of heat transfer. The isothermal process allows the fastest rate of heat transfer.

P. 24
Turbine: Turbine is a device that spins in the presence of a moving fluid. The difference between water wheel or windmill and a turbine is largely one of emphasis and degree. During the 18th and 19th centuries, much progress was made towards extracting the kinetic energy of flowing water by devising water turbines. The term 'turbine' is derived from *turbo*, a spinning object.

P. 29
Transponder: In particular, a communications satellite's channels are called transponders, because each is a separate transceiver or repeater. Older television satellites in the C band have 24 transponders, while newer Ku band ones have 32. With digital video data compression and multiplexing, several video and audio channels may travel through a single transponder on a single wideband carrier.

P. 30
Optical interferometers: Optical interferometers are instruments that can make very precise measurements of objects using the interference pattern of two waves of light. One wave interacts with the object being measured, and the other does not; their interference when they encounter one another allows measurements to within one-thousandth of the wavelength being used. Very small distances and thicknesses can be measured, including extremely small surface irregularities in optical devices such as mirrors. In astronomy, interferometers are used to measure the distances between stars and the diameters of stars.

P. 34
Aphrodisiac: An aphrodisiac is an agent that causes the arousal of sexual desire. The name comes from the Greek goddess of love, Aphrodite. Desire can be stimulated by a variety of events or situations, or through certain foods and drugs. Some aphrodisiacs appear to gain their reputation from the principles of sympathetic magic, e.g. oysters, due to their shape. This also explains the trade in the phallic-looking rhinoceros horn, which is endangering this animal.

Neurotransmitters: Chemicals that transmit information across the junction (synapse) that separates one nerve cell (neuron) from another nerve cell or a muscle. Neurotransmitters are stored in the nerve cell's bulbous end (axon). When an electrical impulse travelling along the nerve reaches the axon, the neurotransmitter is released and travels across the synapse, either prompting or inhibiting continued electrical impulses along the nerve. Neurotransmitters transmit information within the brain and from the brain to all the parts of the body.

P. 37

Cocaine: An alkaloid drug derived from the leaves of the coca shrub. A commonly abused illegal drug, cocaine has limited medical use, most often in surgical applications that take advantage of the fact that, in addition to its anaesthetic effect, it constricts small arteries, lessening bleeding.

P. 38

Venturi: A fluid passing through smoothly varying constrictions experience changes in velocity and pressure, as described by Bernoulli's principle. A venturi is a system for speeding the flow of the fluid, by constricting it in a cone-shaped tube. They are found in many applications where the speed of the fluid is important, and form the basis of devices like a carburetor.

Jacuzzi: This is a brand of bathtubs and saunas. The first product was a bath with massaging jets; the trademarked name is commonly used to refer to any bath with water jets. Those who use them consider them relaxing, but people might accidentally spread diseases when in a jacuzzi.

P. 40

Radiograph: An image produced on a radiosensitive surface, such as a photographic film, by radiation other than visible light, especially by X-rays passed through an object or by photographing a fluoroscopic image.

Electron: An elementary particle carrying a unit charge of negative electricity. Ordinary electric current is the flow of electrons through a wire conductor. The electron is one of the basic constituents of matter. The name electron was first used for a unit of negative electricity by the English physicist, G. J. Stoney, in the late 19th century.

P. 47

International Date Line: An imaginary line through the Pacific Ocean roughly corresponding to 180° longitude, to the east of which, by international agreement, the calendar date is one day earlier than to the west.

P. 48

Bazooka: In warfare, portable, lightweight metal tube from which rockets are launched, usually operated by two men. The bazooka is used by infantry as an anti-tank weapon and also for attacking pillboxes and bunkers. In general, the bazooka is a short-range weapon with low accuracy; however, it gives the individual soldier the means of destroying heavily armoured vehicles and fortified positions.

P. 51

Dichroic glass: In the last several years there has been a growing interest in the use of dichroic glass. It is used to create 'pretty baubles' that will sell! Dichroic is in the 90s, what silver chloride was for hot glass blowers in the 60s, an easy way to add colour and intrigue to the piece of glass.

Teleidoscope: Teleidoscope is a kind of kaleidoscope. The main difference between the two is that the teleidoscope has a lens and an open view. A teleidoscope uses a clear sphere or lens instead of beads, and the observed image is broken into repeated segments. This results in kaleidoscopic patterns deriving from real objects, rather than predetermined visuals.

P. 52

Equinoxes: Either of the two points on the celestial sphere where the ecliptic and the celestial equator intersect. The vernal equinox, also known as "the first point of Aries", is the point at which the sun appears to cross the celestial equator from south to north. This occurs about March 21, marking the beginning of spring in the Northern Hemisphere. At the autumnal equinox, about September 23, the sun again appears to cross the celestial equator, this time from north to south; this marks the beginning of autumn in the Northern Hemisphere. On the date of either equinox, night and day are of equal length (12 hour each) in all parts of the world; the word equinox is often used to refer to either of these dates.

P. 53

Hydrophilic: Hydrophile, from the Greek hydros or water and philia or friendship, refers to a physical property of a molecule that can bond with water. A hydrophilic molecule is one that typically is electrically polarised and capable of hydrogen bonding, enabling it to dissolve more readily in water than in oil or other 'non-polar' solvents. Hydrophilic molecules can establish hydrogen bonds with water molecules (H2O). This is favourable by thermodynamics and makes these molecules soluble in water.

Presbyopia: A condition that occurs with growing age and results in the inability of the human eye to focus on objects up close. Presbyopia is most likely the result of a decrease in the flexibility of the lens of the eye, changes in its curvature from continual growth, and loss of power of the ciliary muscles (the muscles that bend and straighten the lens). Presbyopia is not a disease as such, but a condition that affects everyone at a certain age. The first symptoms are usually noticed at the age of 40-50. It can start with difficulty reading fine print, particularly if the lighting is poor, or with eyestrain when reading for long periods.

Astigmatism: A type of faulty vision caused by a non-uniform curvature in the refractive surfaces — usually the cornea, less frequently the lens — of the eye. As a result, light rays do not all come to a single focal point on the retina. Instead, some focus on the retina while others focus in front of or behind it. The condition may be congenital, or it may result from disease or injury; it can occur in addition to nearsightedness or farsightedness. The patient observes a pattern of straight lines placed at various angles, those running in one direction appear sharp while those in other directions (particularly at right angles to the sharp lines) appear blurred. A special cylindrical lens is placed in the out-of-focus axis to correct the condition.

P. 54

Kayaks: Eskimo canoe, originally made of sealskin stretched over a framework of whalebone or driftwood. It is completely covered except for the opening in which the paddler sits. Since the paddler wears a waterproof skin-shirt which is laced to the boat, he can turn all the way over without sinking. The kayak is propelled by a double-bladed paddle and is primarily a hunting canoe. Because of its maneuverability in ice-infested waters, it is still in use over a great extent of the Arctic.

P. 55
Perchloroethylene: A colourless, non-flammable organic solvent, Cl2C:CCl2, used in dry-cleaning solutions and as an industrial solvent.

P. 56
Integrated circuits: An electronic circuit built on a semiconductor substrate, usually one of single-crystal silicon. The circuit, often called a chip, is packaged in a hermetically sealed case or a non-hermetic plastic capsule, with leads extending from it for input, output, and power-supply connections, and for other connections that may be necessary when the device is put to use. Integrated circuits can be classified into two groups based on the type of transistors they contain. Bipolar integrated circuits contain bipolar junction transistors as their principle elements. Metal-oxide-semiconductor (MOS) integrated contain MOS transistors as their principle elements. Some integrated circuits contain both types of transistors.

P. 60
Vacuum pump: A rotary claw-type, positive displacement pump designed for either pressure or vacuum applications. It is available as a single-stage or two-stage vacuum pump. Vacuum or pressure is provided by two non-contacting, claw-type rotors in an oil-free chamber. Wearing parts are thermally separated from the pumping chamber, leading to longer pump life. Because of wide variable speed range, they are adaptable to many applications in a broad range of industries.

P. 61
Crankset: The component of a bicycle drive-train that converts the reciprocating motion of the rider's legs into rotational motion used to drive the chain, which in turn drives the rear wheel. It consists of a set of chain-rings, the crank-arms. It is connected to the rider by the pedals, to the bicycle frame by the bottom bracket, and to the rear sprocket, cassette or freewheel via the chain.
Sprockets: A device like a wheel with one or more rows of teeth-like parts sticking out which keeps a chain moving on a bicycle or pulls film, paper, etc. through a machine.

P. 62
Chlorination: Chlorination is the process of adding the element chlorine to water as a method of water purification to make it fit for human consumption (potable). Water which has been treated with chlorine is effective in preventing the spread of disease. The use of chlorine has greatly reduced the prevalence of waterborne diseases as it is effective against almost all bacteria and viruses.

P. 63
Magneto-dynamic: The magneto-dynamic propulsion system is an electromagnetic space propulsion system somewhat similar to an ion engine. It utilises a magnetic field functioning as a 'magnetic nozzle' to confine the accelerated gas.
Cardioid: The cardioid is an epicycloid which has one and only one cusp. That is, a cardioid is a curve that can be produced as a locus by tracing the path of a chosen point

of a circle which rolls without slipping around another circle that is fixed but which has the same radius as the rolling circle.

P. 64
Gyroscope: A device consisting of a spinning mass, typically a disc or wheel, mounted on a base so that its axis can turn freely in one or more directions and thereby maintain its orientation regardless of any movement of the base.

P. 65
Subatomic: The only subatomic particles found in ordinary atoms are the electron, proton and neutron. The space or orbital(s) containing the electron or electrons makes up the bulk of an atom's volume. The configuration (and consequently the behaviour) of the electron(s) is responsible for the chemistry of atoms; an electron has 1/1836 the mass of a hydrogen atom and a negative charge.

P. 66
Penicillium soil mould: Penicillium mould are occasional causes of infection in humans and the resulting disease is known generically as penicilliosis. Penicilliosis is an infection caused by Penicillium marneffei, a dimorphic fungus endemic to Southeast Asia and the southern part of China. Persons affected by penicilliosis usually have AIDS.

P. 67
Chromatic: Able to refract light without spectral colour separation. It pertains to colour.
Magnification: The act of magnifying or the state of being magnified. Something that has been magnified; an enlarged representation, image or model.

P. 68
Monotype: Monotype refers to a taxonomic group with only one subgroup at the next (smaller) taxonomic level; for example, a monotypic genus has only one species. A monotype in the text of this book refers to the printing process in which each and every letter of the word is printed individually, i.e. a unique print made by pressing paper against a painted or inked surface.

P. 69
Condensing chamber: A condensing chamber is a tank into which air may be compressed (or condensed) to do experiments. The air is pumped into it using a condensing syringe.

P. 70
Exothermic process: Exothermic process is one that transfers heat to the surroundings. An exothermic reaction feels hot. The most obvious effect of an exothermic chemical reaction is a rise in the temperature of the reaction mixture.

P. 71
Dispenser: A dispenser is an automated machine that can provide something already stored in it, when spurred by human operator. This 'something' could be cash, coffee or anything else depending upon the purpose for which the machine is installed. Spurring could happen by electromagnetic card or coin or an ID card.

P. 72

Clone: Group of organisms, all of which are descended from a single individual through asexual reproduction, as in a pure cell culture of bacteria. Except for changes in the hereditary material that come about by mutation, all members of a clone are genetically identical. Laboratory experiments in in vitro fertilisation of human eggs are being conducted.

Binary fission: Binary fission is the a sexual reproductive process used by most prokaryotes, which results in the reproduction of a living cell by division into two equal, or near equal, parts. Binary fission begins when the DNA of the cell is replicated.

P. 73

Micro-organism: A micro-organism is an organism that is so small that it is microscopic (invisible to the naked eye). Micro-organisms are often illustrated using single-celled, or unicellular, organisms; however, some unicellular species are visible to the naked eye, and some multi-cellular species are microscopic. The study of micro-organisms is called microbiology.

P. 75

Spherical bearings: Spherical bearings offer an unequalled combination of high load capacity, high tolerance to shock loads, and self-aligning ability, but they are speed limited. Accordingly, spherical bearings are used in vibrators, shakers, conveyors, speed reducers, transmissions, and other heavy machinery. Although the majority of spherical bearings are made to RBEC-1 tolerances, high-precision grades are available.

P. 76

Serendipitously: Serendipity is normally used to refer to finding an interesting or a valuable thing or phenomenon just by chance.

P. 77

Semiconductor: A solid state substance that can be electrically altered. Certain elements in Nature, such as silicon, perform like semiconductors when chemically combined with other elements. A semiconductor is halfway between a conductor and an insulator. When charged with electricity or light, semiconductors change their state from nonconductive to conductive or vice versa. The most significant semiconductor is the transistor, which is simply an on/off switch.

P. 78

Nuclear fission: In physics, fission is a nuclear process, meaning it occurs in the nucleus of an atom. Fission is when the nucleus splits into two or more smaller nuclei plus some by-products. These by-products include free neutrons and photons (usually gamma rays). Fission releases substantial amounts of energy (the strong nuclear force binding energy).

P. 79

Vacuum: A vacuum theoretically is the space without matter in it. A perfect vacuum has never been obtained; the best man-made vacuums contain less than 100,000 gas molecules per cc, compared to about 30 billion billion (30×10^{18}) molecules of air at sea level. The most nearly perfect vacuum exists in intergalactic space, where it is estimated that on the average there is less than one molecule per cu m.

P. 80
Phenakistoscope: The phenakistoscope was an early animation device, the predecessor to the zoetrope. One variant of the phenakistoscope was a spinning disc mounted vertically on a handle. Around the centre of the disc was drawn a series of pictures corresponding to frames of the animation; around its circumference was a series of radial slits. The user would spin the disc and look through the moving slits at the disc's reflection in a mirror.

P. 83
Trinitrotulene: In its refined form, trinitrotoluene is very stable, and unlike nitroglycerine, it is insensitive to friction, blows or jarring. This means that it must be set off by a detonator. It does not react with metals or absorb water, and so unlike dynamite can be safely stored for many years. It is however readily acted upon by alkalis to form unstable compounds that are very sensitive to heat and impact.

P. 85
Interface: An interface is a specification that exists between software components that specifies a selected means of interaction, by means of properties of other software modules, which abstract and encapsulate their data.

P. 86
Conveyor belt: A conveyor belt consists of two end pulleys, with a continuous loop of material that rotates about them. The pulleys are powered, moving the belt and the material on the belt forward. Conveyor belts are extensively used to transport industrial and agricultural materials, such as grain, coal, ores, etc.
Cleats: A strip of wood or iron used to strengthen or support the surface to which it is attached to a projecting piece of metal or hard rubber attached to the underside of a shoe to provide traction and cleats. A pair of shoes with such projections on the soles. It is also a piece of metal or wood having projecting arms or ends on which a rope can be wound or secured. It is wedge-shaped piece of material, such as wood, that is fastened onto something, such as a spar, to act as a support or prevent slippage. It is a spur like device used in gripping a tree or pole in climbing.

P. 87
Hydraulic: A branch of engineering concerned mainly with moving liquids. The term is applied commonly to the study of the mechanical properties of water, other liquids, and even gases when the effects of compressibility are small. Hydraulics can even be operation by or involving the pressure of water or some other liquid.

P. 88
Fulcrum: A fulcrum is a term used to describe a part of a percussionist's grip that is the main lever for the stick/mallet to rotate. This is usually created by the thumb + index finger, the thumb + middle finger, or a combination of the index finger, the middle and the thumb.

P. 89
Gnomon: An object, such as the style of a sundial that projects a shadow used as an indicator. The geometric figure that remains after a parallelogram has been removed from a similar but larger parallelogram with which it shares a corner.

Escapement: The escapement drives the pendulum in a pendulum clock, usually from a gear train. The gear train is powered to provide energy to the pendulum, typically using springs or weights. Without the escapement, the system would simply 'unwind' immediately, but the escapement stops this motion periodically, controlled by the pendulum.

P. 91
Reconnaissance: Reconnaissance is the military term for active gathering of information about an enemy, or other conditions, by physical observation. It is part of combat intelligence as compared to counter intelligence.

P. 92
Neanderthal: The ancient and now extinct relatives of modern humans. Neanderthals lived in Europe about 150,000 years ago and were the earliest form of the human species, Homo sapiens. The term 'Neanderthal' is sometimes used to refer to a person who is thought to have primitive or unenlightened ideas: "I tried talking politics to Joe, but he's a real Neanderthal."

P. 93
Configuration: In communications or computer systems, a configuration is an arrangement of functional units according to their nature, number, and chief characteristics. Often, configuration pertains to the choice of hardware, software, firmware and documentation. The configuration affects system function.

P. 94
Joystick: A pointing device used to move an object on screen in any direction. It employs a vertical rod mounted on a base with one or two buttons. Joysticks are used extensively in video games and in some CAD systems.
Simulator: One that simulates, especially an apparatus that generates test conditions approximating actual or operational conditions. It is a machine that simulates an environment for the purpose of training or research.

P. 95
Ethanethiol: Ethanethiol is a colourless liquid that has a strong odour, resembling that of rotten eggs. The odour is familiar to many people who use natural gas and propane for cooking and heating, as it is used as an additive to give those normally odourless fuels a distinctive smell.

P. 96
Galvanised: To stimulate or shock with an electric current; to arouse to awareness or action; to coat (iron or steel) with rust-resistant zinc.

P. 97
Penstock: Penstocks are intake valves to control the flow of water in water supply, hydroelectric power and sewerage systems. Penstocks are normally equipped with a gate system and a surge tank. Flows are large with a major portion of the water supply flowing through the penstock system. Flow in penstocks is regulated by turbine operation and is nil when turbines are not in service. Control strategies include hot water wash, manual cleaning, anti-foulant coatings and desiccation.

P. 99

Polycarbonate: Polycarbonates are a particular group of thermoplastics. They are easily worked, moulded and thermoformed; as such, these plastics are very widely used in modern manufacturing. They are called polycarbonates because they are polymers having monomer groups linked together by carbonate groups in a long molecular chain.

Silk-screening: Screen-printing, also known as silk-screening or serigraphy, is a print-making technique that creates a sharp-edged single-colour image using a stencil and a porous fabric. A screen-print or serigraph is an image created using this technique.

Fold here

Fold here

Fold here

Fold here